the Secret
BOOK BOYFRIEND

ELLIE HALL

About this book

Can this shy bookstore owner who's never been kissed turn the grumpy hockey-playing beast who owns the building into a book boyfriend, er, book lover?

Vohn

I'm good at two things: playing and coaching hockey. Not a businessman, when I inherit a prime piece of real estate downtown, the plan is to level it to make room for a parking lot. Anyone else hate fighting to the death for a spot?

Gracie

I have two dreams: open a bookstore and find a guy who is a swoony sweetheart like the heroes in my favorite novels. As for Once Upon a Romance, achievement unlocked. I'm officially ready to match readers with the books they love.

Vohn

I get caught breaking into my building by a woman wielding a dictionary. Can't lie. She's adorable in those pajamas. I like what I see. Too bad I have to kick her out.

Gracie

My new landlord is a grump and a brute. Who hates books? Him. That's who. Pages fly when we clash, but things heat up when we get stranded during a storm.

Vohn

Plot twist. Turns out I need her help and she needs mine, so I propose a fake marriage of convenience.

Gracie

Didn't see that coming, but like in love stories, maybe if he's my first kiss, he'll turn into a prince.

If you enjoy clean, closed door, small town, grumpy sunshine romcom, then it's time to meet Gracie and Vohn in this instalove standalone novella.

The bookstore you'll find between these pages Once Upon a Romance is for you, dear reader. It may be a fictional oasis for book lovers, but I hope you find it would make a great gathering spot for our very own book club.

A Note from Ellie

Hello! I'm so happy that you picked up *The Secret Book Boyfriend*. If you're new to me as a reader, I extend a warm welcome to this sweet and swoony world! Get ready for quirky humor, silliness, feel-good moments, occasional sniffles, and a happily ever after.

For those who have been with me for a while, you'll know that I've created several grumpy sunshine couples, but this is my first encounter with insta love which is similar to love at first sight. In most cases, the couple's affection for one another grows gradually, perhaps stemming from a shared past, or it can develop as a slow-burn realization of their deep emotions.

I gave instalove a shot for a fresh writing experience and to keep it a shorter read. Well, it turned out a little longer than I intended and there is a bump in the road when the main characters "meet." I hope you enjoy Gracie and Vohn's falling in love adventure!

If you're in the mood for more hockey romance after this, check out the Nebraska Knights series. Additionally, I have numerous other romantic comedy series that include large families, brothers, enigmatic wills, treasure hunts, quaint towns, tight-knit friend groups, daring dating challenges, cozy coffee shops, holiday themes, cowboys, billionaires, and much more!

Don't forget to keep an eye out for my weekly newsletter. I like to think of it as a love note for book lovers. It includes writing updates and author news, freebies and deals, excerpts, and MORE! If you don't see it, check your spam/junk, promotions, or social tabs on your email provider.

In the meantime, snuggle up with Gracie and Vohn's story!

Hugs,

Ellie

August

From: <FantasticMr.Foxx@email.com>
To: <BookShopGirl@email.com>
Date: August 16, 4:31 PM
Re: 4th Street store rental

Dear Ms. Cadell,

Thank you for your inquiry into the available rental space. You seem like a lovely young woman with a bright vision for your business. Opening a bookstore in Cobbiton would be a great addition to the town. I'd be happy to lease the space to you on one condition.

You like books, so I assume you're also good with words. You may rent the building if you send a monthly email to this address: NumberThirtyThree@email.com.

Your note can be positive, thoughtful, or sweet. A few kind words of encouragement. That's all. Please do not mention me. Don't ask for personal details or share your own. Consider it a good deed for a good cause—a way to pay it forward to someone who needs to be reminded of the sunshine every once in a while. He hasn't smiled in years, which I think we can both agree is a travesty.

Attached, you'll find the rental contract. If the terms are agreeable to you, please sign, date, and return it at your earliest convenience.

All my best,

F. Foxx

~

From < BookShopGirl@email.com >
To: < FantasticMr.Foxx@email.com >
Date: August 16, 4:49 PM
Re: 4th Street store rental

Dear Mr. Foxx,

Thank you for this opportunity. My jumping for joy probably just set a world record. This is a dream come true. I wish I could express to you what this means to me without sharing my life story.

The additional sprinkle of email mystery adds to the excitement. I'd be happy to send a monthly note to this anonymous NumberThirtyThree account.

I signed the contract and attached it below. I'm looking forward to adding to the literary enrichment of Cobbiton so thanks again. And although it's a little unusual, I'm seizing the opportunity to make someone's day a little better once a month by doing that favor you requested.

Warmly,

Gracie Cadell

From < BookShopGirl@email.com >
To: < NumberThirtyThree@email.com >
Date: August 19, 10:02 AM
Subject: Warm Greetings!

Hello! As they say, I'm just going to yeet it! Full send. Jumping right in here with warm greetings, and to let you know that today is a good day to appreciate the sun—even if it's not shining it is still up there—and eat a grilled cheese sandwich. Oh, and have dessert. Maybe have dessert first. Cupcakes make everyone smile. Ice cream too.

Salutations!

-BSG

P.S. Do you like rainbow or chocolate sprinkles? Cup or cone? Sugar or cake or waffle?

Me: rainbow, cup, waffle bowl!

From < NumberThirtyThree@email.com >
To: < BookShopGirl@email.com >
Date: August 19, 12:02 PM
Re: Warm Greetings!

Maybe you sent this to the wrong person. Thought you should know because your message was unique and unusual—didn't want it to go unanswered.

Also, it's cloudy today. No sun in sight. But (grilled)

cheese is yellow, though I'm more of a ribs guy with barbecue sauce. Not much of a fan of dessert.

#33

September

From < BookShopGirl@email.com >
To: < NumberThirtyThree@email.com >
Date: September 22, 1:10 PM
Subject: Welcome autumn!

I'm definitely in the right inbox and on a secret, special, and anonymous mission to make you smile, so thank you for replying!

It's fall, y'all! I'm not Southern, so I hope it's okay to use that expression. I couldn't help myself. Oops, I'm not supposed to share personal details. Too late now. I'm not going to use the backspace key. I guess now you know that I live in the United States.

I love autumn, spring, and summer. It might be an unpopular opinion, but I like winter too! Never met a season I didn't like. The changes with each one are a great reminder to let go, to rest and renew, and above all to have fun! That looks different for different people. For instance, my idea of fun is curled up with a book, my cat, and some tea. How about you? Also, what's your favorite season?

-BSG

P.S. Yes, grilled cheese sandwiches are my favorite. Not a big ribs fan, though. So you really don't like dessert. Not even ice cream?! I'd like to change that!

From < NumberThirtyThree@email.com >
To: < BookShopGirl@email.com >
Date: September 29, 5:51 PM
Re: Welcome autumn!

I have no good reason to reply to emails from a stranger, but I don't want to be rude—which, just being honest, might be a first for me. I'm not known for my manners.

Since you asked, I never really thought about my favorite season. I suppose winter for sports and stuff. But I wouldn't say no to a tropical getaway right now. Just for a few days. Is it sunny where you are?

#33

October

From < BookShopGirl@email.com >
To: < NumberThirtyThree@email.com >
Date: October 12, 9:22 AM
Subject: Spooky season!

Hi #33,

It's always sunny where I am! I take it with me wherever I go. LOL. I would love a tropical getaway! I've never been to a place with palm trees.

So you don't like dessert? Fine, I suppose we can still be friends. Does that mean you have a salty tooth instead of a sweet tooth? I'm a snacker. Snacks forever! And chocolate. Also, I would never turn down a piece of Halloween candy. What's your favorite kind of Halloween candy? Wait. Maybe you don't like it either. Weirdo. Just kidding. Totally joking. I'm giving it out this year and dressing up as Alice in Wonderland. By telling you that now you know

- I live in the United States

- How I like my ice cream
- I'm female
- My Halloween costume

How about you? Er, you don't have to tell me about yourself. But if you want to, you can share your Halloween costume or party plans. Maybe you're hiding in your basement?

I'm rambling. In real life, I'm pretty introverted. People say I'm shy. But talking over email is easier for me. And this little assignment has been surprisingly fun! A nice break from my busy days. I hope your Halloween is filled with treats and no tricks!

-BSG

P.S. Happy Haunting!

~

From < NumberThirtyThree@email.com >
To: < BookShopGirl@email.com >
Date: October 15, 7:11 PM
Re: Spooky season!

Is there an Ebenezer Scrooge equivalent to Halloween? If so, that's me. Holidays shmolidays. This begins my busy season, so I can't promise to stay in touch. As for candy, I avoid the stuff, but if a Sweet Tart fell into my mouth, I wouldn't spit it out if that answers your question.

Hope you have some leftover chocolate and don't get too spooked by kids in their costumes.

#33

~

From < BookShopGirl@email.com >
To: < NumberThirtyThree@email.com >
Date: October 30, 6:22 PM
Re: Spooky season!

Happy Halloween Eve! Your email made me LOL. Don't worry, I stashed some chocolate in case the trick-or-treaters clean me out. I hope your busy season goes smoothly. Can't lie. I'm curious about what you do and who you are, but I'll keep things simple and say hello again next month.

But before I go, have you ever wondered about plastic *silver*ware or *jumbo* shrimp? Like how can they be both? It's not that things like this keep me up at night, but I guess I notice and wonder... How about you? Anything on your mind? Musings? Notable moments to share?

-BSG

P.S. Holidays, even the not-serious ones like Halloween, can be hard for people. You'd think that would be the case for me. My parents were holiday (and book) enthusiasts. I lost them when I was a kid and was raised by my uncle whose actual name is Ebenezer, if that tells you anything.

~

From < NumberThirtyThree@email.com >
To: < BookShopGirl@email.com >
Date: October 31, 9:30 PM
Re: Spooky season!

Confession: I went to the store and picked up a package of candy. Not to give out because I'd probably scare away the kids but to have on hand should I get a craving. I blame you. You're a bad influence. Half the bag of fun-sized treats is already gone. Thanks for ruining me.

#33

P.S. Super sorry to hear about your parents. I don't know how to say it better than that, but that's a sucky thing, and Uncle Ebenezer? Bah humbug. You seem like the kind of person who would've done better with Mary Poppins or Maria from the Sound of Music. I didn't say I've seen those movies, but my family moved to the US from Germany when I was a little kid and my mom watched them all the time to help her improve her English. It was hard not to get those songs stuck in my head. Just saying.

∼

From < BookShopGirl@email.com >
To: < NumberThirtyThree@email.com >
Date: October 31, 9:35 PM
Re: Spooky season!

Think of my influence as an enhancement. There's no such thing as being too sweet. But like I was saying in my last email, what about *bitter*sweet? How does that work? I need answers, people!

As it is, we're entering the season of eating with the holidays coming up. I've been busy, but I'm also hoping this is a busy season for my business too. I sure need it.

Without giving too much away, I own a store, and even though there isn't any direct competition in my town, because it's pretty niche, there is in the wider world, and it's cutthroat. I thought the hardest part about opening would be all the administrative paperwork to make sure it's operating properly.

However, the challenge has been getting people's eyeballs on the place. Considering it's Halloween, that sounds a little odd. I've had so many customers say, *I had no idea you were here*!

How do small businesses get the word out these days? If you know the secret sauce, please share. Though, I have no idea what you do, so it might be on another spectrum entirely.

Anyway, wish me luck, and you as well! We got this. My emojis are glitching, but I tried to do the high-five one.

-BSG

November

From < NumberThirtyThree@email.com >
To: < BookShopGirl@email.com >
Date: November 1, 6:22 PM
Re: Spooky season!

Status update: Less than twenty-four hours later and the candy is gone.

   #33

∾

From < BookShopGirl@email.com >
To: < NumberThirtyThree@email.com >
Date: November 1, 6:30 PM
Re: Spooky season!

Bwah ha ha ha! Mission accomplished. Next up, ice cream. I'm coming for you #33!

   -BSG

P.S. Does this count as my monthly good deed note? Or can I send another one? It's kind of fun having an email pen pal!

P.P.S. Which do you like better, books or movies?

~

From < BookShopGirl@email.com >
To: < NumberThirtyThree@email.com >
Date: November 24, 11:00 AM
Subject: Thankful Hearts!

Happy Thanksgiving, #33! I assume you're in the US and celebrate, but if not, happy Regular Thursday! In any case, there's a lot to be thankful for. Here's my list (in no particular order and it's not exhaustive, but I don't want this to be too long):

Cozy blankets

Coffee

Bible study

Books

Long walks

YOU!

I suppose we're just anonymous acquaintances, but having someone to chat with about anything and everything is a welcome break from the hustle. I'm going to be really candid here since we don't know each other in real life, and may never meet, but getting an email from you makes my days a little less lonely.

I'm not a shut-in or anything, and I have good friends, but I've never dated. The few people I've told don't believe me. But it's true. I've never been asked out. Not when I was in school and not once since. To give you a sense of the timeline, I went to my ten-year high school reunion last year. Also, now you know about how old I am.

Oh, and I should also say I'm not hideous or anything. Furthermore, I'm aware we live in the modern era and I could certainly ask out a guy. No big deal, right? But as I mentioned, I'm a bit shy. Sometimes painfully so. Could be because I was an only child. Do you have any siblings? I can turn "on" when around people, but then I need a nap to recharge. Yes, sometimes literally.

This is all probably TMI (too much information), and I'm kind of rambling. Earlier, I went to my friend's house for a few hours, visited, and had turkey (and pie!), so now I'm home alone again, and it's, well, kind of lonely. I think I'll watch the Sound of Music since you mentioned it. I love that movie!

I do have a cat. Are you a cat, dog, or other pet kind of guy? I'm assuming that you're a man based on context clues, but if I'm wrong, you can let me know. Or not. Okay, I'll stop now.

-BSG

P.S. What's one thing you're thankful for?

From < NumberThirtyThree@email.com >
To: < BookShopGirl@email.com >
Date: November 30, 1:22 PM
Re: Thankful Hearts!

Hey. Sorry. I've been swamped. A lot going on and none of is it good. That's not true. You're right. There is a lot to be grateful for. It could be worse. I won't bore you with the details, but if you're the prayerful sort, I could use one for December 27th. It's kind of make-or-break it for me. I'll spare the details, but it's been a rough few months in my personal life.

#33

P.S. Your notes are definitely a bright spot, so please keep at it, and thank you.

P.P.S. In case you're wondering, my heart wasn't broken per se. Okay, maybe a little bit. More like my trust was shattered. I'm a dude so not really great about talking emotional-type things. It's not a stereotype. It's a biological reality. Sure, we might need opportunities to sort some things out, but it's best done physically. Not like I punched out the guys my ex cheated on me with. Okay, a couple of them saw my fist. But more like taking a long hike would set me right. Or playing a rough game. Too bad I threw that away.

My life blew up and I added gas to the flames. I was upset, disappointed, hurt. You know? I thought, well, I don't know what I thought. But not that I'd be here, on the other side of marriage, of the plexiglass—not like in jail. I mean the kind above the boards— of what I thought my future would look like.

Strange as it sounds I feel like I can trust you. I mean, you have no idea who I am so how could you possibly crush me the way she did? Looking back, that's sort of ironic. She knows loads of personal things about me—my weird pregame rituals, that I can't sleep with socks on, that I obsessively floss.

Guess you know that now too.

But that's not it. She could've humiliated me in really obvious ways. Instead, she went behind my back. Gutted me.

It all leads me to think that I wasn't enough.

Sorry, I'm rambling, but I'm clicking send because it felt good to get that off my chest. Now I'm going for a run and shaking off the residual venom from that woman.

December

From < BookShopGirl@email.com >
To: < NumberThirtyThree@email.com >
Date: December 1, 9:35 PM
Re: Thankful Hearts!

I'm sorry to hear you're in a rough patch. It will get better. Thanks for trusting me. It means something to bring your troubles to the light—sunshine, am I right? I hope it was helpful.

From what I've learned about you, it's not worth it to wonder whether you were enough. Seems to me that she had some stuff that was going on. I don't mean for this to sound like I'm minimizing your situation, but as they say, art imitates life... Or is it the other way around? I can never remember. But in this situation, it might apply. So please hear me out. Here goes:

I read tons of romance books and a lot of times, one or both of the characters has a deep heart wound and ends up hurting the other person because they're hurting. It really doesn't have to do with anything their significant other did, but they end up being on the firing line. What I'm trying to say is that maybe it was her and not you.

And before you say something like, *Yeah, yeah, yeah. You're just trying to make me feel better or something.* Possibly I am, but I also might be right.

Not knowing the details, all I can say is trust things will turn around and this experience—as unpleasant as it is—will bring about some good in your life even if you can't see it now. And I'm sorry if that's hard to hear right at this moment, but it can help to remember that. Also, I keep you in my prayers, but I'll add a prayer that things get better.

I really, truly hope you have a non-Ebenezer Scrooge-lousy-ex holiday season because Christmas is coming! So is winter! My favorite and yours, respectively.

If I were to write Santa a letter, I'd tell him that I've been a good girl and that I'd like books under the Christmas tree. How about you? Or not, you don't have to tell me. I imagine you'd ask for whatever you have going on to resolve. But to shed a little light on the subject, just for fun, what was the coolest gift you got as a kid? Or if you could travel back in time (and were Santa Claus—roll with me here), what's something you'd give your younger self?

There are certain books that I read more than once. So for me, I'd want signed original copies of all my favorite books. I've been collecting them in the years since, but I'd like to round out my collection even though tracking them down is part of the fun. I know, I know. I'm a book worm through and through.

Let's see, maybe I can take your mind off things. Would you rather:

Live in a big city or small town? (Me: small town near a big city)

Get gifts under the tree or have an experience? (Me: can I say both?)

Cider or hot cocoa? (Me: hot cocoa with extra cream and chocolate shavings)

Christmas cookies or cake? (Me: cookies)

Last one: Grinch or Elf (Me: Elf!)

-BSG

P.S. If I don't hear from you before Christmas, no worries. I hope it's merry and memorable!

From < NumberThirtyThree@email.com >
To: < BookShopGirl@email.com >
Date: December 30, 1:22 PM
Re: Thankful Hearts!

I'll skip the update on everything that happened, but it's over. I think. Thank goodness. Am I relieved? I'm just hoping I'm out of the danger zone. Don't worry, I didn't break any laws or anything like that. Also, I'm like an ox. Nothing gets me down or stops me.

A while back, you mentioned that you're an only child and are shy. You seem pretty outgoing to me. I have three siblings, and my brother is kind of like that. If you get to know him, he's a total goofball, but when around new people, he's pretty quiet and reserved. My parents are still happily married. Guess that skips a generation (which also may give you a clue to what I've been dealing with).

I hope you had a merry and memorable Christmas and that Santa brought you lots of grilled cheese sandwiches, books, and chocolate but not all at once. That would be weird. Here are the answers to your Would You Rathers:

Live in a big city or small town? (Me: same)

Get gifts under the tree or have an experience? (Me: experience)

Cider or hot cocoa? (Me: cider)

Christmas cookies or cake? (Me: who has Christmas cake? Weird.)

Last one: Grinch or Elf (Me: Grinch 100%)

#33

P.S. See you next year. I mean, email you next year!

January

From < BookShopGirl@email.com >
To: < NumberThirtyThree@email.com >
Date: January 1, 12, 9:35 AM
Subject: New Year Same Me!

Happy New Year! I hope it's filled with good health, cheer, and cake. I don't know who eats Christmas cake, but cake is good for all occasions, like Monday mornings, when you finish painting a wall, or getting through a rough patch (late December for you). I'm glad to hear you're through it. If you ever need to vent, I'm your anonymous email pal!

Cake for all occasions!

Per my Would You Rather, I'd still go with cookies though. Hmm. Maybe a cookie-cake combo? Oh, right, you don't have a sweet tooth (except for the fun-size Halloween candy. Wink, wink).

I'm moving winter higher on my list of favorite seasons because it makes a great excuse to be cozy. There has been so much snow lately! I know it's boring to talk about the weather. At least that's what I've been told. And that I'm socially awkward, but I learned that in some cultures, it's customary to discuss the weather first. Kind of like an icebreaker before discussing other topics.

But if you stop and think about it, how cool is the weather?! It's not something we control and yet influences our lives in such a powerful way. That said, I prefer a sunny day with blue skies, though I'd bet good money most people agree. But because of the contrast of how special those days are compared to foul weather, it makes us appreciate the good ones so much more. Don't you think?

-BSG

P.S. If you could have any superpower, what would it be? Mine would be to fly because I bet it's really peaceful up with the birds.

February

From < BookShopGirl@email.com >
To: < NumberThirtyThree@email.com >
Date: February 14, 2:14 PM
Subject: Love Month!

I hope this isn't weird, but happy Valentine's Day!
    -BSG

March

From < BookShopGirl@email.com >
To: < NumberThirtyThree@email.com >
Date: March 21, 9:19 PM
Subject: Spring has sprung

It's officially spring! The birds are chirping, but the flowers aren't blooming. Not yet. My favorite are gerbera daisies. I'm not telling you that because of the Valentine's Day thing, what with flowers and chocolates being customary gifts. I hope my last note didn't freak you out.

   -BSG

   P.S. Don't forget to set your clocks forward!

From < NumberThirtyThree@email.com >
To: < BookShopGirl@email.com >
Date: March 31, 2:45 PM
Re: Spring has sprung

My apologies! I did reply to your last note, but it was stuck in my outbox. But I'm glad because I was a cornball and wrote a cheesy joke. Redacted.

Though, I'll admit I like corn and cheese so I'm not sure why they're associated with dorky things.

The clouds haven't quite parted in my life yet (it's been pretty rainy here), but it feels like all that stuff will soon be in the past (and my team is doing pretty well this season).

Your emails make me think that maybe all these showers will bring some spring flowers. Haha. Okay, so that was corny too, but not as bad as the joke which, in hindsight, I'm glad didn't go through.

Following up on a few things:

I'm a cat guy. My mom loves them, so it must be genetic.

My superpower would be X-ray vision, but not because I'm a weirdo. More like to see through all the thick clouds to the sun, like you said in your first email.

Also, I'd probably go as a superhero for Halloween, since you asked before.

Thank you for the offer to vent. I'm choosing the not-think-about-it-ever-again road.

Movies or books? As if that's even a question. Sports highlights, obviously.

I hope your spring is springing!

#33

GRACIE

AS MY FINGERS trail the spines of my favorite books lined up neatly on the shelves, I'm starting to worry that true love is fictional. It's merely a made-up fantasy by the creative minds of hope-filled writers drunk on romance.

Or it could be that I'm not a main character, fated to find my one true pair.

With a sigh, I flip around the *open* sign to my bookstore, Once Upon a Romance.

It's ten AM, and unless I'm doing a coffee and tea tasting event complete with a BYOP (bring your own pastry, muffin, scone, or breakfast baked good), it's usually slow this early in the morning.

But the bell to the glass-paned door opens. A woman with curly hair that's somewhere between brown and gray enters. She inspects the tidy space as if seeking health code violations.

"Good morning," I say brightly. "Can I help you find the perfect book?"

I've been working on coming up with a bookstore-branded greeting. Of course, the regular time of day welcome is customary, but I want to come up with a slogan that visitors to the store will associate with Once Upon a Romance. Maybe I could even make stickers or put the catchy phrase on tote bags. So far, nothing has stuck.

The woman carries a clipboard. "I'm looking for the owner."

Raising my hand like I've been called on in class, I say, "That's me."

"I mean of this building."

"Oh, that would be Mr. Foxx."

"I see. I'm Nancy Linderberg, chair of the Cobbiton CAC." She has a narrow mouth, and her voice is brisk, like that of a drill sergeant. However, the way she says CAC makes me worry she has a hairball like Janey gets from time to time.

I tilt my head, not sure what that means. "It's nice to meet you. What's the—?"

As if I'm dumb for not knowing the meaning of the acronym, she says, "Community Activities Commission. We're planning the 4th on 4th and want to confirm the use of the sidewalk in front of the building."

"I'm Gracie and relatively new to Cobbiton. This will be my first here. Is that a Fourth of July event?"

"It's one of the biggest in the state. A celebration of our country's independence combined with our corn heritage. We host a street fair that includes a parade, food trucks, big Cobbiton beach, and—"

"I've heard about that. It's like a ball pit but filled with popcorn kernels."

She nods. "There's also a rodeo, talent show, cooking

contest, and polka dancing. We crown an annual Corn Queen, and, of course, there are fireworks."

Sounds loud and busy, which isn't my preferred environment, but it could mean more business, which I desperately need. "I have Mr. Foxx's email address. That's how we communicated for the lease."

"Thank you." She sniffs as if this is an imposition and looks around. "Would you like to contribute to the CAC? We'll include your shop's name on the 4th flyer as one of our sponsors."

My laptop dings with an email notification. An itsy bitsy flutter rises inside with the hope that it's an email from my secret book boyfriend—it's silly, but he's kind of the guy of my romance novel dreams. However, the surge just as quickly falls away because Nancy is asking for money, something in short supply at present.

Even though I'm new to this suburb of Omaha and running a business, I know how these things work. If I don't donate, I'm not a team player and likely rumors will spread. If I do, that means Janey and I might have to go to Free Sample Sundays at the Cost-Club bulk shopping store to save on our weekly food expenditure.

My parents used to say *Our wealth comes from our words* and I'm surrounded by books, but I invested everything I had into this shop and money is tight.

Answering Nancy, I say, "I'd like to. Do you have a website or—?"

"You can make a check out to the Cobbiton Activities Commission for any dollar amount."

My stomach swims with nerves because I can't afford this, but I suppose it's the price of doing business. Maybe with the shop's name listed as a sponsor, I'll get more traffic in here.

I ask, "What do new businesses typically offer?"

Nancy purses her lips like I'm wasting her time. "Fire and Ice, the new Sports Coffee and Beverage Bar, offered five hundred dollars."

I wince. "I'm sorry—"

She wears a tight smile. "I understand."

"No, I want to donate, but," I try to explain registering my business, obtaining insurance, and all the hidden costs beyond books.

"If you change your mind, you can visit our offices at the end of 4th Street."

I nod as she exits, feeling defeated and deflated. It's not that I don't want to contribute. I do, but my budget is down to the cent at the moment.

I took an online quiz recently and learned that my strength is being deliberative—it took me eight years of dreaming before I turned Once Upon a Romance into a reality. I'm also disciplined, empathetic, and focused.

I like to concentrate on the positives and not how, at times, I can feel painfully shy and be somewhat passive. My uncle also criticized me for being naïve and a daydreamer. I guess that makes it hard for me to tell people like Nancy Linderberg no. I get flustered and clam up.

Then I remember the email notification. I hope it's from #33. Mr. Foxx asked me to send an anonymous email to someone once a month. When he made the request, for a second I thought it was him since we'd never met, but I'm certain it's not. It might sound strange, but #33 and I have become friends, and I look forward to our exchanges.

Even though I'm generally introverted and the few customers who come in each day fill my socializing cup, the emails hit different. It's like having a close friend. Sure, I have my besties—Meg and Kara—but my #33 is like a traditional gentleman, torn from the pages of one of my classics, aka my secret book boyfriend, as I've come to think of him.

I open my laptop, but the inbox notification is for a sale on cat toys. "Sorry, Janey. Not this month."

She hops into my lap, and I give her head a little scratch.

For all my life, I've had two dreams: open a bookstore and find a guy who is as swoony a sweetheart as the heroes in my favorite romance novels. As for Once Upon a Romance, achievement unlocked. I'm officially here to match readers with the books they love.

For part two, as I scroll through the exchanges between #33 and me, I feel a tiny bit of pining. I sell purely fiction, including traditional and indie-published books, along with select bookish items like bookmarks, magnets, stickers, and mugs. I'm hoping to get into more merchandise at some point. It's all romance and so far, I haven't had any of my own off the page.

The shop has one big picture window overlooking the street that intersects Main here in Cobbiton—a suburb of Omaha. In front of the window, I put two cushy chairs. The entry door is to one side with another door that leads upstairs to my apartment. Along one wall, there's a bistro table, an old wooden desk, and another small sitting area. I'm hoping to boost the Cover to Cover book club nights from being a three-person meeting with Meg and Kara to a bigger event complete with a charcuterie board. Think olives, cheese, homemade sourdough crackers, fresh fruit, and fruit-infused sparkling water.

But those are someday dreams. My problem isn't a lack of ideas but the resources to fund them. I also have a system for matching readers with the perfect book, depending on their mood, preferred trope, length of book, and several other factors, but I haven't been getting much foot traffic. I'd blamed the winter weather, and so far it's been a rainy spring, keeping people inside.

I check my email again in case a message from #33 fell into the junk trap. If we'd lived in the nineteenth century, we'd write long letters to each other while he served overseas and then have a tearful reunion. My gaze drifts to the special edition copy of Pride and Prejudice. I'd even settle for a Mr. Darcy.

But alas, I'm alone and always have been.

That night, Janey settles on the end of my bed, and I fire up the reading app on my tablet. Yes, I love physical books with paper, but my digital copy of Pride and Prejudice has all my favorite scenes and quotes highlighted.

No sooner have I read the part when the Bennet sisters see Mr. Bingley from the window than I get sleepy and yawn. When I was a kid, I'd read under my covers with a flashlight so my uncle wouldn't catch me. I'd also say good-night to all my books. Once, I even got to do a summer reading program sleepover at our local library. I always wanted to spend the night in a bookstore.

Given the fact that I'm living in the apartment above

Once Upon a Romance, if I really wanted to, I could sleep downstairs—though I avoid the creepy basement at all costs except when we get tornado warnings.

"Ow." I jolt, realizing I dozed off and dropped my tablet on my face.

Janey startles and jumps off the bed, annoyed with me.

After clicking off the light, I roll over and then hear something. A scratching sound coming from somewhere in the building—and it's not the cat. She's back on the bed, circling her spot to snuggle up.

Listening, I worry that there's a rodent in the building.

"Janey, that's your job," I whisper.

The sound comes again, followed by a shuffling noise.

Alert, I sit up, tossing off my blankets. It's spring, but it's still chilly at night. However, I break into a nervous sweat. My pulse drums in my ears.

Is someone trying to break in? Maybe Nancy Linderberg is exacting revenge because I didn't donate to the CAC.

Now, there's a scrape. A shiver works along my spine. Back under the blankets, I quietly dial emergency, whispering into the phone. Then I slip out of bed. I scramble around to find something heavy, blunt, anything I can use as a weapon if need be. The massive dictionary I'm guilty of using as a doorstop will have to do. I clutch it to my chest like a shield.

There's nowhere in my room to hide, so I exit to the hallway. Originally, this used to be a small apartment, but years ago, Mr. Foxx converted my room into an office. The bathroom and a second small room are off the open living area that leads to a stairwell going directly to the outside door.

A large figure fills the fogged glass at the foot of the stairs. He's over six feet tall and has broad shoulders. I can't tell if he's wearing burglar gear like a ski mask. But he's definitely breaking in.

The moment the door swings open, I reflexively throw the dictionary at the intruder and run.

Two

VOHN

NO SOONER DO I open the door than a large book lands at my feet. At the same time, the flashing lights of a police cruiser temporarily blind me.

A grunt escapes.

"Some welcoming committee," I mutter.

If I had my way, I'd retreat to a cabin somewhere remote with a barn I could convert to an indoor rink so I wouldn't have to bother with shoveling the snow. I'd have a wood-burning stove, a constant coffee drip, and a cat to keep me company.

Shielding my eyes, the officer shines his cruiser's spotlight on me. "Stop and put your hands up."

I obey but say, "Sir, there has been a mistake."

"Keep your hands where I can see them." It's then I recognize Adam Ballard's voice.

"Hey, it's me—" I start.

At the same time, he asks, "Vohn? What are you doing?"

"I'm not breaking, but I am entering the building *I*

own." I don't need to explain myself. However, it was dark and my phone was dead, so I didn't have a flashlight. I couldn't figure out which of the twelve keys on Fred's keychain opened the door.

"I didn't realize you were back in town. Good game against the Storm. Baldwin's block was so close." He winces. "But Lemon pulled out the stops. He's like lightning. Good job, boys."

"Thanks. Now, if you don't mind..." I gesture behind me.

It was a long flight from North Carolina with me recapping every moment and play from the game against the Storm. Those guys do the ice dirty and are no better off skates. The Knights have integrity, and our D is undeniably powerful. But we biffed an assist and failed to get the puck out of the defensive zone during the second period.

Coach Badazcek is the kind of calm that lets him sleep at night. I'm in it to win it at all costs. This is one reason I struggle with insomnia.

Adam asks, "Wait, did you say you own this place? That means Fred Foxx left it to you and not—?"

He goes quiet, likely out of respect for me and the very public divorce I endured that led to my retirement, disappearance from the hockey world for a time, and my comeback as an assistant coach to the Nebraska Knights.

I nod, wanting nothing more than to go to sleep and forget why I now own a two-story brick building on 4th Street in Cobbiton. As always, my ex-wife did what she's good at: taking. She got the house, condo, the cars, my hockey puck collection, and all my time and money. Everything.

The separation started a few years ago, on my thirtieth birthday. Then Ilyssa dragged out the divorce proceedings, claiming everything was hers. Finally, I conceded but asked for a year to stay in the condo so I could figure out my next move.

To be clear, I bought the condo back during my glory days when I was still single because of its proximity to the arena. After we married and moved into a house, she accused me of bringing puck bunnies there after games. Turns out, she was hooking up with members of the Storm and hosting parties with other teams at my place while I was out of town

Somehow I'm the guilty party and she's the victim— and her best friend's husband was the judge, so there's that.

In a surprise turn of events, Ilyssa's father left me this property. Guess he didn't think of me as the bad guy she portrayed. But my last night in the condo was the day I flew to Carolina for the game, so now I'm camping out here. The deadline to vacate the condo snuck up on me. Don't get me wrong, I'm grateful for this surprise turn of events and the serendipitous timing because I only found out late last week about inheriting the building, but it's not ideal.

From behind me, the stairs creak, and a small voice calls, "Officer, is it safe to come out?"

My head whips around, and I flick on the light to the stairwell, but whoever is up there remains in shadow.

Adam calls, "Sure is, miss. Thank you for your concern, but I'll let you figure this out."

My brow furrows. "Figure what out?"

The woman calls, "Wait, sir. You're not going to cart him away?"

11

"What is going on?" My voice booms.

"Can't say you weren't warned," Adam mutters.

I stab the air in the direction of the stairwell with my finger. "If anyone is going to be arrested, it should be you. First of all, you're illegally in my building."

Adam says, "Technically, it's called squatting, and believe it or not, people who occupy property without permission have—"

Interrupting, I point to the dictionary. "Secondly, you used a weapon against me."

She holds up her hands. "It's a dictionary and was a reflex. I'm sorry. But you were breaking in and—"

Adam's comms speaker crackles and he gets into the patrol vehicle. "Good seeing you, Vohn. If you need any help, shoot me a text."

"Wait," the woman calls.

But Adam slams the door and pulls away.

I realize he must've thought the woman lurking in the stairwell was Ilyssa.

Without his headlights shining, I can see her more clearly. The figure with long limbs and delicate features— admittedly looking adorable in a pink pajama set covered in bunnies with cottontails—is definitely not my ex. Something flickers inside and I grip the doorframe.

Visually, she's the opposite of the woman the guys on the team collectively call the Lizard Witch from Venus. Yeah, they've got my back. As for Adam's comment about me being warned, yeah the guys made it clear that Ilyssa was a man-eater.

Everyone in town, on the team, and in the wider world of professional ice hockey knows that Ilyssa and I had a whirlwind wedding, were the "it" couple for nine months, and then the rumors started.

I didn't want to believe that while I was on the road playing for the Knights, she was having parties in my condo and then later at our house. I didn't want to think my wife would cheat on me with other hockey players and not have me find out about it.

I was dumbfounded when I tried to work things out and she denied it all even though there was social media evidence. Then I was the dummy when we got back together. In my defense, I thought we could patch things up. But was struck absolutely stupid when she turned on me and tried to take me for everything I was worth when she was the one who destroyed our marriage.

I'm not the victim, but I am innocent.

The problem is, she's very convincing at suggesting otherwise, making me feel a fool for falling for her because I'd been warned, the writing was on the wall, and all that.

Bending over, I pick up the dictionary. It weighs at least ten pounds. "You're lucky gravity worked in my favor because this thing could've broken my nose."

"That was the idea," she whispers.

The scent of almonds and lilacs wafts my way as she carefully creeps toward me, arm extended to take back the book.

"I don't bite."

"But you do break into buildings."

As my gaze floats over her, my head spins. Must be tired. My stomach clenches. Hungry too. Even though involvement with women is at the bottom of my list at the moment, I can't deny that I like what I see. Too bad I have to kick her out.

She takes the dictionary and our hands brush. My pulse sprints, but I don't have anything to worry about. She's not dangerous.

Even though downtown Cobbiton is quiet at this late hour, somehow the silence becomes complete except for my raging heart. It's because I now have to deal with more trouble when I thought I'd finally wiped off the muck of the last several years.

Soft brown eyes wide and clutching the dictionary to her chest, she walks backward, taking one step at a time like a scared animal. I'm certainly not going to hurt her. This is the kind of woman that men who're worth the name would protect, provide for, and die for.

Giving my head a little shake because I thought I dispatched those notions during the divorce, I keep my hands where she can see them. However, because I have no business indulging these thoughts, my approach to the situation and my tone harden in equal measure when I ask, "Can you explain why I shouldn't throw you on the street?"

Her full lips drop into a frown and she sputters, "Because—"

Just then, a fluffy white cat races toward us, gaze glued to the open door.

"Please, close the door. Janey, stay inside." The plea in her voice is so desperate that I block the cat in, which means that I'm now sealed in the stairwell with this woman.

I'd only been to Fred's office once, shortly after Ilyssa and I were engaged. He said he started his empire here, working all hours as a small firm insuring corn farmers. He then added commodities like oil and gas before expanding to become a nationwide entity. This means his daughter was spoiled, which didn't help me. Looking back, the short, round, and bald man with a polished dome also warned me about Ilyssa. In so many words, he told me his daughter was trouble and always got what she wanted—just like his ex-wife.

If only I'd listened when he said that it's important for a man to look after his corn, every kernel. I'm only now building back my bank account. Not that money is everything. But Ilyssa made sure every cent was painful to hand over.

I don't remember this space with its wood paneling running up half the wall and the rest in need of fresh paint being so small. My breath doesn't quite hit the bottoms of my lungs when I take a deep breath. Man, I'm tired.

The cat winds its way around my legs. I crouch down to scratch its head. Ilyssa was allergic to cats. My mom had two —Kitty and Cat. Not too original, but they kept her company when we kids grew up and moved out. I appreciated them because they were a lot like me. Independent and interested in attention on an as-needed basis.

"Don't kick her," the woman says.

My head snaps up. "What? Why would I kick your cat?"

Biting her lip and holding the dictionary in front of her chest like a shield, she says, "In books, the hero saves a cat, but the villain kicks a cat. Well, usually not literally, though sometimes..."

The white cat sits on the step between us and licks its paw like it's preparing to mediate this conversation.

Scrubbing my hand down my face, I say, "Listen, I just got in after a long flight. I don't want to be a total jack-wagon, but this is my property and—"

She gasps. "You're Mr. Foxx?"

Shaking my head, I start to correct her.

Ignoring me, she plows ahead. "I thought you'd be older. White hair, a distinguished beard, perhaps." She tilts her head as if painting a picture. "Smaller for sure. Maybe a little paunch from enjoying a scone slathered in clotted cream with your afternoon tea."

Tucking my chin, I say, "Mr. Foxx is best described— was best described as..." I hold my hand up because the guy was scrawny and had pointed features, much like his daughter. Recently, she had all kinds of surgical enhancements, thanks to my funds which she took.

A long sigh escapes. I'm over it. Completely done with Ilyssa unless she rears her ugly head. I don't care if that makes me sound like a villain. She went too far with the cosmetic alterations and looks like a lizard trying to masquerade as a human, hence the name Lizard Witch from Venus.

On the other hand, this willowy woman with sweeping eyelashes, lush lips, and a locket resting between her collarbones is an all-natural beauty. Something flares inside, but I turn my attention to hockey: ice, twigs, and pucks can't betray a guy.

At last, I say, "I am not Mr. Foxx, but I do own this building."

"Then who are you?" she asks with a tremor in her voice.

I've been wondering that a lot lately because my life hasn't turned out exactly as I hoped.

"He never said anything about it changing hands. In fact, I haven't heard from him in months. Not since our original email exchange." She narrows her eyes, scrutinizing me. "If you own this building, tell me what's in the basement."

"A monster."

She snorts a shaky laugh. "Nice try. If you own this building, you'd know the special request Mr. Foxx had in order for me to lease it. What is it?"

"Pay on time." He was a stickler for punctuality.

"Duh. But there was something else. A secret smile mission as it were."

A sneaking suspicion slides into my mind. I'm exhausted, yet the pieces tumble together and then scatter. In their place, comes the imaginary girl of my dreams. BookShopGirl. She was sweet, relatively normal, and reminded me that my entire life wasn't a battleground. But now is not the time to think about things I cannot have and don't deserve.

This woman standing on the stairs eyes me with caution. The muscles in my neck tighten with tension. This could very well become a problem, and I've had enough of those for a lifetime.

Three

GRACIE

THE SUSPECTED INTRUDER, with broad shoulders and a toned body, hulks at the base of the stairwell. It's important for me to profile him even though I'm not clear on why the police officer left. Do I look like I can handle this situation by myself? The answer is no.

In case I need to provide a detailed description later, I make note of his dark brown hair. It's tousled in the front, sweeping his heavy brow. His stormy gray eyes are intense and I avoid them, my gaze darting around the small space.

If I were a romance writer instead of a reader, his full lips would be best described as kissable. The dimple in his chin is manly. He sports stubble, suggesting he needs a shave or is one of those guys who goes for the rugged look. Also, he smells like cedar. However, I don't suppose the police sketch artist would need to know that.

With authoritative confidence, he says, "I'm Vohn Brandt, and I own this building."

Exhausted and confused, my knees give way, and I drop onto the step. Janey gives me a side eye, reminding me that even though I avoid confrontation and conflict at all costs, I might want to remain standing for this.

"If you're not Mr. Foxx, but you do own this building, who did I email?"

"That's your primary concern right now?"

"Obviously. Was I conned?" If I can't trust Mr. Foxx, how could I possibly trust #33? My book boyfriend dreams are dashed.

"I assure you, there is no trickery going on."

"You're not the Mr. Foxx I envisioned. More like a beast of a man."

Granted, this beast of a man is foxy if you're into that kind of thing, but he's also an outrageously rude grouch.

With a snort, he says, "Of greater importance is that you're breaking the law."

Holding my head in my hands, I mutter, "Says the guy who broke in."

"What am I missing?" His voice is low, gruff.

"My question exactly. If Mr. Foxx doesn't own this building then who have I been paying? I signed the lease—" I opt to leave out the email part. "Was I scammed?"

He grunts. "No, but there was no mention of a tenant."

"He and I never met in person, just corresponded via email." I knew it was risky, but easy enough to overlook since my bookstore dreams were coming true. I practically have our correspondence memorized because I read it so many times before agreeing to Mr. Foxx's unusual request. He wrote that I could rent the building if I did him a favor.

Vohn presses his lips together and mutters, "And here I thought the clouds were finally parting."

I tip my head from side to side. "Mr. Foxx seemed

slightly eccentric." I stop myself from saying more about the email request because it sounds slightly nutty now.

"There was no love lost between him and his ex-wife or his daughter," Vohn says darkly and then adds, "I'm sorry to be the one to tell you this, but Fred Foxx passed away not long ago and left the property to me."

Even though Vohn doesn't share the last name with Mr. Foxx, meaning he's not his son, they must've been somewhat close.

"How sad. I'm so sorry." I pat his arm with comfort and a shockwave runs through me, heating me all over.

He shrugs me off, and I fold my hands in front of myself.

This brawny beast of a man glares at me. His fingers splay and then flex.

The motion sends a flutter through me, but I do my best to keep my expression neutral. Knowing me, later on, I'll think of the exact way I could have responded to this situation and what I should have said. I'm a master of after-the-fact responses.

Clearing my throat, my hope plummets. "Mr. Foxx and I had an agreement. I rent the bookstore and the space above for storage."

"You had an agreement with Fred. Did he say you could live up there?" With a massive, manly hand, he points behind me.

He brushes my shoulder, sending a rash of heat across my skin. "I read the lease agreement forward and backward. It didn't say I *couldn't* live up there. And given my financial situation, it's all I can afford. I poured my life savings into Once Upon a Romance. Statistics suggest most new businesses bear a financial loss during the first year. I have three months until, hopefully, things move in a positive direction."

I sense Vohn's gaze on me, so I risk looking up. My cheeks blaze. His eyes flick from wonder to disbelief, confusion—I'm not sure what—and land back on stormy.

"Can we talk about—?" My smile falters when he interrupts.

"How about not? I'm exhausted." He lets out a long breath. "I'd rather discuss this after I've had some sleep and coffee. Just got in from the East Coast. Long weekend and an even longer flight after some delays due to bad weather."

This whole night feels oddly like a scene out of a novel that's hitting the dark moment when all is lost. I imagine myself on a steamer ship, waving goodbye, but instead of holding a kerchief, it's like each page of my Once Upon a Romance story falls into the sea.

GRACIE

VOHN SHIFTS from foot to foot and I half expect an earthquake. "I was expecting to crash here tonight and need a place to sleep. I'd go to a hotel, but they're booked for the corn convention. I can't sleep in my car because I don't have one. Took a Zoomber rideshare from the airport."

Shadows fill my mind with too many questions to count. Biting my lip, I say, "You can sleep in the other room if you're okay with the floor. There's a couch in the basement, but I couldn't get it up here by myself." Clearing my throat, I add, "But, um, my boyfriend is a real beast, so if you try anything, he'll—"

Vohn's eyebrows lift on his forehead. "If you had one of those, you would've called him and not the police."

I shrink and hug my arms around my chest. "Story of my life," I mutter. It's not that I need a boyfriend, but I've never had one period, which leaves me feeling lonely and wondering what I'm lacking.

"The floor is fine."

"How do I know you are who you say you are?" I ask.

With a grumble, he flips open his wallet and shows me his license—Vohn Fitz Brandt resident of Nebraska and a November baby. I also glimpse several hundred-dollar bills and credit cards.

"Satisfied?"

An exhale lurches out of me. "Fine. But whatever you do, please don't let out Janey."

"The cat?" he asks.

"Yes, Janey Pawsten author of Purred and Prejudice." I gather her into my arms.

If Vohn were a normal person, he'd chuckle slightly at the play on words, or at least the corners of his stormy eyes would crimp with amusement. Instead, he stomps up the stairs after me.

If Vohn were a regular guest, I'd make sure he had everything he needed, including bath towels, linens, and a mint on his pillow. Instead, I give him a quick litany of where everything is as he gawps at the books and boxes that fill the main room—overstock and some collector copies that I have been saving for most of my life. I want a shelf dedicated to original editions, but that'll come later.

"Good night," I say.

He simply nods.

I lock the door to my bedroom and keep the dictionary close in case I need to defend myself. Janey snuggles back into her spot instead of standing sentry like a guard cat.

As I lie in bed, my thoughts swirl. I wish I'd seen Mr. Bingley out the window instead of Mr. Grumpy. This development makes me feel bleak, but then why hasn't the fluttery warmth inside gone away?

Having a veritable stranger in the other room makes me

want to implode with fear but curiosity explodes inside me, too.

The police officer didn't seem overly concerned about my safety, so I tell myself everything is fine. I'll wake up to the birds chirping and the sun shining just like every other day.

Just so I can sleep, I tell myself that Vohn is my book boyfriend and we're going to fall in love. I pretend that, like #33, he has three siblings, likes Sweet Tarts, and is a sports enthusiast. Oh, and the whole thing about his shattered heart promises that he'd never break mine—not like how Vohn was breaking into the building. I mean, he owns it and all, but details, details.

It's been a long time since I've shared a place with someone. Even if it's strange and crazy and possibly dangerous, the idea of a beast in the next room makes me feel a little less alone.

The cover of darkness gives me courage, and I call, "Are you awake?"

A rumbly grumble sounds in reply.

"Please don't murder me."

I know he's not in the room with me because I turned on my LED flipping pages book night light, but the walls are thin and I startle when his voice floats close in reply.

"I'm not that kind of beast," he growls.

"Thank you for sparing me," but I don't think he hears me because a loud snore comes from the other room.

~

The next morning, I sleep past the normal time. Blinking open my eyes, I recall why I'm eye level with a dictionary.

The night floods back, and I'm no closer to feeling settled about the events than I was when I finally fell asleep.

After pulling on a robe, I peek into the living space. The door to the other room is partly open. Thankfully, the hulking man with the perma-frown is gone.

I exhale with relief, fingers crossed that I imagined the whole thing.

However, there are traces of Vohn; the scent of cedar fills the air, the sink is damp, and a rumpled towel fills the bottom of the wicker laundry basket. A strange and stark disappointment leaves me wondering about the whole secret book boyfriend thing.

After a short walk to Busy Bee Bakery to grab a latte, though today it should be a double, I open Once Upon a Romance for business. Within the hour, my phone beeps with a flurry of texts. It's from the group loop I share with my friends Meg and Kara.

> Kara: Mrs. Gormely has been hooting all morning about how the police performed a raid on your shop and that you're involved in a burglary ring.

> Meg: Do you need backup?

I'm not sure whether to laugh or find a rock to hide under. By the way, I've never understood that expression. If a rock were big enough to hide a human under, wouldn't it squish them?

> Me: Thanks for checking in. To be honest, I'm not entirely sure what happened, but Janey and I are fine.

> Kara: That's a relief.

My cat curls up in a patch of sunshine coming through the big front window.

> Kara: But was there a midnight intruder?

> Me: Yes. No. Sort of. I'm still unclear what the story is, but he's gone.

Hopefully, for good.

> Meg: I'll pretend that made sense. Nancy Linderberg told Mrs. Gormely that you didn't want to donate to the CAC for the 4th Fest. I can spot you.

> Me: That's generous. Thank you. It's not that I didn't want to contribute. But I'm watching my business budget.

Counting every single penny.

> Kara: Generally, I don't pay much attention to what those two busybodies have to say, but this just came in. The burglar was none other than Vohn Brandt.

> Meg: The only way I can connect those dots is that he inherited the building from Fred Foxx or is exacting revenge. I'll ask Micah. For those outside the Knights bubble, Vohn is a retired top player and now an assistant coach.

Had we not started discussing the Fred Foxx connection, I'd go with a revenge plot as his motive, given the guy's general stature and demeanor.

> Kara: Micah is great, but if I had to choose, I'd go with Vohn every single time.

> Meg: I'll pretend you didn't say that.

There's no denying that both men are attractive. However, Micah and Meg are happily married. I don't know Vohn's status and am ready to forget about the man with masculine features and firm muscles. I hardly even noticed the way they stretched his T-shirt or how he stood with squared shoulders and casual confidence. *Pfft.* Who cares about that?

> Kara: Let me get this straight. You and Vohn Brandt had a midnight encounter. Have you seen him? He's very tall. Wink, wink. Don't tell me you're not throwing your hat into the Micah versus Vohn ring.

> Me: Yes, I saw him breaking into my building last night. Then, um, he slept in the spare room.

The girls know that I can be a bit insecure about my height. I'm not a giant by any means, but guys are rarely taller than me. On the upside, it means I reach books on the top shelf.

Vohn could get the ones that even I can't reach. That would be handy. A flare that runs through me at the memory of his proximity to me in the stairwell stains my cheeks pink even though I'm alone and there's no one to see —like usual. Granted, I have my best friends, but they're busy with their lives. Meg is married, a mom, helps with Junior Explorer Scouts, and designs hockey lover merch that she sells online as a side hustle. Kara is a software developer for a startup and works insane hours.

> Meg: I'd pick Micah all over again. He's a thirst trap snack.

> Kara: Do you know what that means?

Spending a lot of time on social media, promoting my store, means I do. I'd argue that neither is true. No offense to Micah.

> Kara: I'll explain. It's a simple chemistry equation. Sometimes you want a slowly simmered marinara sauce and other times you're okay with pre-made out of the jar.

> Meg: I'm ignoring you. Moving on. Reports suggest you threw a shoe at Vohn.

And sometimes Kara says things that only she understands. I'd have failed high school chemistry had it not been for an amazing tutor. I'm no good with science, but when it comes to literature and grammar, I'm your girl.

Me: It was a dictionary.

Kara: Speaking of shoes, what do we think about these fashion Crocs?

She shares a photo of bright green Crocs with a high heel instead of the regular foam sole.

Kara: Kind of fun, right?

Meg: Ghastly.

I agree, but before I can say so, Vohn thunders into the shop. When I meet his stormy eyes, my body rebels, and I blush. The flutters inside are like pages in a book, but I warn myself that this one won't have a happy ending. Not with this brute of a man involved.

Five

VOHN

AFTER SLEEPING in what amounts to a closet, I got up while the dawn was still gray and hit the ice. It's the only thing that reliably clears my head.

Some people think that coaches stay comfortable in the warm room on the safe side of the glass and no longer play hockey. While that might be true for some assistant coaches, there's nothing average about me.

I train with the guys, hit the puck hard, and can still keep up with the pros. If it were me against the opposing team during sudden death, I'd crush them.

When I left the arena, the sky was blue, and I pulled the fresh spring air into my lungs. I needed it to prepare for my visit to the bookstore to tell the owner the bad news.

But it must be done.

When I walk in, a bell on the door jingles. The cat greets me with a sleepy stretch. To be fair, I didn't look carefully at the information the lawyer sent me regarding the property and had no idea there was a tenant. Gracie Elizabeth Cadell, signer of the lease, is much more than I expected, especially considering I wasn't expecting anyone.

But I won't go there because while I may still be decent at hockey, I'm trash at relationships and romance. Which may as well be this woman's middle name.

She appears from the back with a few books clutched to her chest. Thankfully, it's not the thick dictionary. That thing could do real damage. Her, too—especially to the brick walls I've built around myself. The mortar is still drying.

"Good morning. Can I be your reading matchmaker?" Her voice is light, and her smile is bright like sunshine.

It nearly stops me, but Newton's first law—an object in motion remains so at a constant velocity—is in play. I'm like a bulldozer, moving slowly closer.

She adds, "I'll help you find the book of your dreams."

I say, "I'm not looking, and I don't need your help."

Her expression falls. "I take it you didn't like my greeting. I'm still working on it. Was it too much? Maybe I should be more casual. Let customers approach me if they need help. I don't want to be salesy or overbearing. I certainly don't like when employees hover, but I'm trying to be inviting and friendly. Plus, it's hard not to be excited because I love books and—"

I hold up my hand to end her rambling because it only makes this harder.

Before I can speak, she presents a paperback with a couple on the cover. "You might like this one. It's a romantic suspense and—"

"I'm not here to buy a book."

"You look like you just got bad news." She bites her lip

as if not sure how to deal with me. Or is she intuitive and senses what I'm here to do and skirts around it at all costs?

Bulldozer, full steam ahead. "I'm here to deliver bad news." Guilt scratches at my chest, promising to torment me later if I go through with this, but I have to stick with the plan.

This woman's overall positivity, the way she becomes passionately animated with her eyes brightening, and her never-fail smile when talking about books aren't doing me any favors.

"Bad news?" Her expression is a slow-motion plummet as her smile falls.

"Obviously."

If I looked up the word *naïve* in that gigantic dictionary of hers, I'm afraid I'd find her face would be on the page. If there's a thesaurus around here, she'd also be under the entry for *hopeless romantic* or *sweetly innocent*; she's the kind of woman who could turn a man with a stone heart into a softy. I can't afford that.

"Should Janey sit down for this?" she asks.

I arch an eyebrow.

Her lips quirk. "I'm joking."

Great. She also has a sense of humor. My sister has a high-pitched laugh anytime someone shares a tragedy. She doesn't mean to be inappropriate. It just happens. Gracie probably saw what's coming the moment I walked in the door and is doing her best to avoid the inevitable. Turns out, me, too.

I mutter, "You don't have to be so cheerful all the time."

"And you don't have to play the brooding tortured

hero." As if in complete denial, she says, "Before I forget, the back door seems to be out of plumb. I think so anyway. I looked it up online. I kind of have to lift it by the handle to get it to close properly. Seems like bad weather causes the wood to expand, making it worse. That's what the internet suggested."

Yep. She's definitely playing dodgeball with me.

"And that's my problem because...?"

Her eyes widen. "Because you're my landlord."

Nostrils flared, I inhale, drawing on patience. I am not noticing how smooth her skin is or how graceful her movements are. Nor am I enjoying her gentle voice or her lilac almond scent.

"Reports also state that you're an assistant hockey coach. That's cool. You know, with the *ice* and all. Everyone loves the Knights. Big fans here in Cobbiton. Apparently, for the 4th on 4th Fest this summer, they're making a mosaic of you guys out of different colors of corn kernels. Neat, right?"

Brushing my hand down my face, I mumble, "I'm going to need more coffee for this."

Gracie bounces on her toes and says, "Today is your lucky day, my good sir. I got samples from a local roaster. I'm hoping to offer coffee and tea tastings once a week. I mean, if that's okay with you."

"No, I mean, yes. No." I shake my head because she has me out of sorts. Maybe I was wrong about her being naive. Perhaps she's obnoxiously optimistic.

Ordinarily, when I walk into a room, there's a sudden hush because I take command—that's but one of the reasons Coach Badaszek was all in with me joining the team as a coach. The guys respect me because of my history on the ice. If not that, they're intimidated by me. Either way, I win, which means the Knights do too.

This has been true with two exceptions: my ex-wife when emboldened by her lawyer to drag me through the mud and now Gracie. I don't need this in my life right now.

I open my mouth, but she cuts across me, saying, "So about the door, since you're the businessman landlord, and do manly, lordly things, I figured you could help me fix it."

"I'm not."

"You're not what?" She tilts her head in question, causing the ends of her long hair to part and expose her collarbones. An ornate, vintage style locket nestles there, drawing my gaze and making me wonder more about this woman than I ought.

My jaw tics. "I'm not a businessman or a landlord."

"But last night...so you are a criminal?! I'm calling the police." She thrusts her finger at me.

I hold up my hand. "I own this building, and that's what I came here to talk about."

"So let me get this straight. Mr. Foxx left—"

"Fred."

"Mr. Foxx left you this property."

"Yes, Fred is my ex-wife's father. I was the son he never had, or so he said."

The inner edges of her eyebrows pinch together like she just got bad news about her cat.

I wave my hands dismissively. "This whole thing was an offside call."

"Is that legalese?"

"Yes, no." Why does she have me so rattled? "It's a hockey term."

"Make this make sense."

I don't want to seem like the villain of the story and find myself holding my breath. But this must be done. "Fred left me the property, but now you have to get out."

"Get out?" she asks so slowly I almost change my mind.

"Yes, the plan is to level the building to create overflow parking for the arena."

Her delicate throat bobs on a swallow. "I figured you'd hate cats, but it's books you despise."

"I didn't say I hate books."

"You're a selfish, spoiled beast-man." Her head bobbles with each word.

I want to laugh because she's right. But laughter and smiles have been in short supply lately. The guys on the team routinely try to get one or both out of me, but it's like my face and funny bone quit on me.

I hold Gracie's gaze. It's not the same way I'd confront some idiot who thought he'd win a fight against me on or off the ice. No, it's like she's challenging me to the depths of my being—demanding me to get clear on who I think I am and what I'm doing here.

I murmur, "You're too bubbly and bright for your own good."

"Who asked you? Are you the pessimistic police? The dreary dream dasher?"

"Call me whatever you want except landlord."

"You really want me to close my bookstore?"

I can't waver or cave. I have to stick to the plan. Gritting my teeth, I answer, "I really do."

Her lips fall into a frown, and liquid pierces the corners of her eyes. Ilyssa tried to ply me with fake tears of apology after cheating on me with numerous guys. My defenses rise, and like Newton's law of motion, I won't let Gracie bulldoze me with some pity story.

"You're one of those hopeless romantics. Once upon a time, they fell in love, and lived happily ever after. The end. Blah, blah, blah."

She sniffs, and then her eyes dart from side to side like she missed something crucial to the conversation. "Well, yeah. Of course. But the story wink is *the end* is actually *the beginning* of the happily ever after," I grind out.

Before she can add color to that lie, I say, "Story wink?"

"Yeah, the story wink. It's an extra little nod that points to the truth of hope, love, and trust." She winks, and I experience internal combustion.

"There is no such thing as love or happily ever afters."

Brown eyes soft and full of empathy, she asks, "Who did this to you?"

"Did what?"

"Ruined you so completely. You're jaded, cynical, brooding—"

Folding my arms in front of my chest, I say, "I didn't ask for a character portrait."

"Consider it complimentary, free, on the house. You can take one of these stickers too as a souvenir." She speaks with a smile as if nothing, not even my lousy mood, can dim her glow. But it's a mask. She's in denial.

When I delivered the bad news, Gracie wore a heart-shredding expression. The fraction of warmth that still exists in me wants to soften, but I'm sticking to the plan and not letting her stop me. I let that happen once, and Ilyssa ruined me.

Never again.

GRACIE

THE MOMENT VOHN walked into the bookstore this morning, I felt like Belle, facing down the beast. A big, broody creature who's incapable of smiling. He didn't even crack when I joked about my cat needing to sit down for the bad news.

My first thought was, *Someone woke up on the wrong side of the bed, er, floor this morning.* My second was, *Be brave, Gracie!*

I'm generally an agreeable person. Some say I'm a pushover. When things get hard, my instinct is to turn and run, not to square my shoulders and face intimidation.

Yet that's what I'm doing. Mostly. My chin is up, and I'm not wavering from Vohn's stormy gaze even though I'm wobbly inside.

Despite how flustered I feel—flustered and warm all over—he is a guest in my shop. Vohn is also my landlord, but I'll let that situation remain foggy for now. One challenge at a time.

A mixture of sadness and anger prick my heart. I've had

so much taken away from me. I won't let go of this store, my first-page dedication to my parents, so easily.

Bracing my hands on the checkout counter, I say, "Usually, in books, the main character has a problem, and the love interest swoops in to save the day. It could be to rescue her cat or save her shop."

His expression goes from one part storm to equal parts stone to ashen. "Are you saying you're the main character?"

I nod vaguely before realizing what the rest of my statement with the love interest sounded like. "I mean, yes, no. Those are the basic roles. But it could be the other way around." I cringe because that's not much better. "I don't mean to say that either one of us is the love—"

"Has anyone ever told you to quit while you're ahead?"

The urge to stomp my foot is strong. "Yes, that has come up. One person, in particular, told me not to dream so big. Yet, here I am, and Once Upon a Romance is a reality. Also, I disagree with you about there being no such thing as true love. However, I have yet to meet a man who even comes close to being like a fictional character. Is it so bad not to want my bubble to burst?"

"You're better off living in the real, non-fiction world."

"I don't want any part of that if it's so harsh. What I meant was usually the guy comes in and saves the day. Instead, you're evicting me. *Un*saving the day."

He scratches his temple. "Yeah."

"Yeah? No 'I'm sorry.' Or at the very least an explanation. I followed all of Mr. Foxx's rules, have paid on time, and—"

"I'm putting in a parking lot."

"A parking lot? Here? Where a perfectly good building stands?"

"The plan is to take advantage of hockey fan traffic and parking garage overflow."

"What a terrible idea. And I'm not saying that because I enjoy fighting for a parking spot."

He glowers.

I pick up my phone and do a quick search. Just as I suspected. "Your math isn't mathing, and I'm terrible at it so yours must be worse."

"Explain," he says dryly.

"At most, you'll have forty-one home games per season. How often does the arena's massive parking garage with underground parking for overflow fill up? How many spaces will this lot make available? How much will you charge?"

Wearing a cocky expression, Vohn says, "Maybe half the time. At least fifty spots. Twenty dollars each. Untaxable money."

"That's probably illegal."

"What Uncle Sam doesn't know..."

"Nancy Linderberg and the rest of the nosy Nellies in Cobbiton probably will."

Moving on, I say, "You think the owner of the arena won't expand if they have to send away cars? They can build *up* in case that didn't occur to you. Meanwhile, I pay rent every month with the expectation that at some point you'll raise it, meaning you'll make consistent cash here."

"Don't forget people are always looking for parking during special events in Cobbiton."

My shoulders sag. "But isn't having a thriving downtown shopping district where visitors and locals can support small businesses important?"

"So is making responsible fiscal decisions."

I come out from behind the checkout counter, breezing past Vohn. In the haze of last night in the stairwell, I didn't quite realize how tall he was, towering over me with his broad shoulders and thick arms. Kara was right about his height.

Standing in front of one of the bookshelves, I search for a title. "When was the last time you read a book?"

He shrugs. "Can't remember."

"That's sad. And I'm not just saying that to be righteous. I mean it. Books help deepen our understanding of what it means to be alive. It makes the world bigger because there's so much to learn and it brings us together, making the vast planet with billions of people smaller through the shared human experience. They spark curiosity and cause transformation—"

"That's all very nice, but it doesn't change my mind."

My chest sinks because this kind of confrontation is the precise sort I try to avoid. It's not that I'm passive, well, sometimes I am. More often I'm agreeable. Growing up with my uncle, who was a moody curmudgeon, who silenced me with a sharp look and then sent me to boarding school after I asked too many questions, taught me that lesson fast.

But I don't give up this time. I won't let Vohn take Once Upon a Romance from me without a fight.

"When I'm inside a story, everything glitters and shines. Reading about other people's lives and experiences helps us better navigate the ups and downs of life and can help us be more empathetic. To do better. Be better. See and feel more. Books give us hope."

He snorts. "That's cute, but I have a plan, and I'm not wavering from it."

Just then, thunder cracks outside. The sky darkened significantly from earlier this morning. My phone beeps with a weather alert at the same time the tornado sirens whistle. The hair on my arms lift.

"I expect you to have everything packed up by the end of the month. Good luck." Vohn turns to leave, but the sky breaks with rain. A solid sheet pours down in front of the building.

Clearing my throat, I say, "Also, you need to replace the gutters."

"On May first, a wrecking ball will handle any problems this building has."

"Enjoy the rain...and raining on my parade," I mutter.

This afternoon, I'll reread the entirety of the lease agreement. There has to be a loophole or something to give me time to convince Vohn that his parking lot plan is terrible. Maybe I can talk to Nancy from the CAC about rules against turning a building on one of the main streets of Cobbiton into a parking lot. We can stage a protest. Drive the beast out of town with pitchforks and flaming torches. Okay, maybe that's taking things a bit far, but still. I'm not giving up on my books, and I'm not giving up on hope.

Vohn stands in the doorway, bowed over his phone. Even though a freight train couldn't stop him from rushing outside, it seems the rain gives him second thoughts. Maybe it's because he'll melt. Do beasts, werewolves, or vampires melt in the rain? What paranormal characters am I thinking of? This afternoon would be a good time to curl up with a romantasy.

His shoulders drop on an exhale. I think of my email exchanges with #33 and how you never truly know what's going on in someone's life, so I shouldn't be quick to think this grump's demeanor has to do directly with me. He could have some big stuff going on behind the scenes. Does that make me naïve, dumb, or am I offering grace?

My voice is small, but I use it anyway. "I've never had anyone come in here and not leave with a book and a smile. That's my mission. To make the rain, whether it's inside or out, dry up and bring out the sun."

He lets out an impatient breath.

I snap my fingers. "That's it. I have my slogan. Welcome to Once Upon a Romance, where readers come for a book and leave with a smile."

"Well, I'm not. Zoomber, my car service app, says they're out of service because of the storm." Vohn peers out the window.

"That's not what I meant," I mumble.

My phone beeps with another alert. I check it this time. Sure enough, there is a storm with chances of strong hail and a tornado warning.

"Do you have anywhere to go?" I ask.

"The arena."

"If I had a car, I'd let you take it. I'd better close up here and get Janey. We'll shelter in the basement. You're welcome to come down there, too, if you'd like," I offer against my better judgment.

"I know. This is my building."

I bristle. "Sheesh. You don't need to be rude. But you may want to clean up down there. It's kind of spooky."

His lips purse, and he circles his finger around the room. "Wrecking ball."

Vohn's stubbornness makes my blood boil. It triggers a hidden boldness inside. He makes me feel like I'm on a seesaw. "What a great contribution to the community—destroy an old, quaint brick building that was once an apothecary, a dress shop, and a toy store, in the heart of downtown Cobbiton."

"No one asked your opinion."

"I didn't share it. Merely stating facts."

He grunts. Thunder rumbles as if they're having a contest.

I shut down my payment system and laptop, grab a few books, and turn off the lights. The dim gray skies dumping water from above make me want nothing more than to curl up with a good book, some tea, and my cat.

Vohn occupies a lot of real estate by the door as he stares down the storm. If he weren't so disagreeable, he'd be the exact stature of my ideal book boyfriend—taller than me, fit, and strong.

He also seems to take up a lot of the air in the room, making mine come in shaky spurts.

"Now, if you please, I'm going to lock up, grab Janey, and ride out the storm in safety." And by that, I mean to get this skin-tingling, tongue-tied attraction under control.

He doesn't move.

Nudging past him, I say, "I don't know what your plan is, but you can share my umbrella until I get inside."

"Don't need one."

"In that case, excuse me." With my tote bag containing my books, phone, water bottle, and a bunch of other stuff slung over my shoulder, I pop the umbrella and exit. The door that leads upstairs is outside, next to this one. By my estimates, if I stay close to the building, only half of me will get wet.

The wind catches the door and my umbrella, carrying it away. I shout, but my words are lost in the wind. I could go back into the bookstore, but I'm better off getting Janey and going to the basement.

To my surprise, Vohn acts like a human shield, blocking me from the rain as I unlock the door that leads upstairs.

"You don't have to—"

As I open the same door he was breaking into last night, a flash of white fur streaks past.

"Janey!" I scramble after her.

Vohn's eyes widen as I run into the storm. He grabs me, clutching me to his chest. I wriggle to get free. Not because I want to avoid his strong embrace—the wind is so powerful, I'm at risk of blowing away. Rather, I have to save my cat.

Over the roar of the gusts, I shout, "Let me go. Janey is afraid of thunder and is likely hiding under the Cobbiton Chronicle newspaper box. She escaped twice before, and that's where I found her."

Vohn picks me up, places me inside, and disappears into the heavy rain. Is he rescuing my cat or has he had enough of me? My breath is short, and my stomach churns. Should I go after Janey? I make a deal with myself. If he's not back in ninety seconds, I'm going after my cat.

I start counting, and the thunder and lightning interrupt me. A dark form emerges from the gloom clutching something. If I didn't know better, I'd think it was a football player heading for the end zone.

I open the door, but the wind grabs it out of my hand. It flies back, and before I can duck out of the way, it hits me square in the forehead.

The last thing I see before everything goes as dark as night is a very handsome retired hockey hero, holding my very wet cat.

Seven

VOHN

CRADLED IN MY ARMS, eyes closed, Gracie looks small and vulnerable. I already gave her devastating news about her bookstore that almost brought her to tears. There's no crying in hockey. Apparently, that rule doesn't apply to being a romance bookstore owner. But I couldn't also have blood, er, fur on my hands.

Over the wind, all I caught was her shout that the cat was scared of the storm and that she might hide under the newspaper box. I found Janey easily enough and coaxed her out before the gutter overflowed onto the sidewalk from the pounding rain. Back inside, I figured I'd find an elated Gracie, thanking me profusely and making me uncomfortable with her gushing gratitude. I'm good with a simple, *Thank you, You're welcome* exchange.

Instead, she was on the floor of the stairwell, passed out. Based on zero medical training but countless hours spent around men playing one of the most brutal sports in the biz, I diagnose her with a mild concussion, if that. Likely, she was overwhelmed and had a case of the vapors or whatever women experienced in those old dramas and romance books, not that I'd read something like that.

I find the door under the stairs that leads to the basement. Gracie was right. Well, I wouldn't call it spooky down there, but it's dark, dank, and filled with cobwebs. I set her carefully down on an old sofa where she must've hunkered down during the last storm and take two minutes to tidy up before going back for her cat and some supplies, tossing everything in a bag—not the cat. I carry her in my arms like a man, not a beast.

Thankfully, Janey likes me and doesn't use her claws. Wish I could say the same for her owner with the way she held her ground with me earlier. No sooner are we settled in the basement than she rouses.

Eyes wide, she startles, nearly leaping out of my arms. I clutch her tighter in case she's lightheaded. I don't want her to fall again.

The flare inside when our gazes meet is bright, but I do my best to extinguish it. I'd probably be better off out there in the rain.

"Are you bringing me to your lair?" she asks, voice shaky.

"No. The storm warning was to seek shelter from possible tornadoes. We're in the basement."

"Why am I in your arms?"

"You don't remember," I say dryly. "Your cat escaped, and the door must've hit you in the head. You have a real shiner."

Her fingers lift to her forehead. "I always wanted to try bangs. That would hide it."

"It should heal. I got some ice from your freezer."

"Where's Janey?"

"Hiding under the chair." I tip my head over my shoulder. "I brought some supplies down here. Not sure what you need. Grabbed your tote bag and everything that spilled out of it." I eye a hand-sewn book sleeve that says *No Peeking* on it.

"Don't be judgy. Everyone needs a bookish blind date for Saturday night."

"I'm not even going to ask what that means."

"That's fine because I'll tell you. My two best friends and I have the Cover to Cover book club. It's Meg, who's married, Kara whose dating life could be a novel, and me, who doesn't have one at all," she mutters that last part and picks at her fingernail.

"How does the date part factor in?" I ask despite myself.

"Each month we buddy read a book, but we also surprise each other with one, hidden in the book sleeves that Meg made each of us."

I grunt because Gracie is intolerably cute.

"Thank you for being resourceful and not leaving my cat out in the storm or me in the stairwell."

Tuning out the inner flare when I'm with Gracie is going to require an industrial-sized firehose. "You're welcome."

I pass her an ice pack. Her fingers are a warm contrast when they brush mine, igniting a blaze throughout my body. This is getting dangerous.

The muted wind howls upstairs, but otherwise, the moment passes in silence, maybe because she's surprised by my sincerity and attentiveness.

"I'm not a total beast."

Her eyes twinkle in the dim light. "Yes, you are."

Does that mean she likes that about me? Before I fool myself with that line of thought, I ask, "How do you feel?"

"I feel a big lump. That's not going to be pretty."

In the half-light down here, I have to admit that even with the injury, she is beautiful, and I'm relieved she seems to be relatively okay. Seeing her slumped in the stairwell gave me a scare.

My voice is low, a little rough when I assess, "Does your head ache? Do you feel dizzy?"

"It hurts a bit, but the door hit me when the wind whipped it. I didn't react quickly enough. But I'm not dizzy or lightheaded."

"How many fingers am I holding up?" I lift three.

She imitates me, and her gaze floats past my eyes. I tell myself to resist their pull and how she draws me in like a reader who wants just one more chapter, one more page. See? She's already in my head.

Clearing my throat, I say, "What day is it?"

"The day after we met."

I grunt because of course that's her rainbows and roses, romantic answer. "Last one, are you the kind of person who dots the letter *I* in her name with a heart?"

"Yes. How'd you know?"

"It was a hunch."

"Are you the kind of guy who doesn't know how to cry?" she asks as if that's a fair counterpoint to how she writes her name.

I grind my jaw. "Of course I don't. I'm a hockey player. It's a rough sport."

"Are you telling me there are no tears in hockey?"

"Exactly."

Eyes twinkling, Gracie says, "My turn."

"Your turn what?"

"To ask you questions like people do when they're getting to know each other. Ever heard of icebreakers?" The corner of her lip lifts into a half smile.

"I play hockey, so yeah."

She brushes her hand on my arm and a sensation that's the opposite of ice flares through me. Oh, man. What did I get myself into? Time to put on the brakes before this turns into a conversation. "You just asked me something. I didn't agree to play twenty questions."

"You asked me the date."

"To make sure you're not concussed."

Breezing by my comment, she says, "Do you want to talk about who broke your heart?"

"So, you admit I have a heart?"

She pinches her fingers together. "A small one."

"Very funny."

"But if you want to talk about what happened? It might help."

"You go right for the jugular, huh?"

"That being a vein, I prefer to think of it as getting to the heart of the matter."

"Haha. Very funny." I don't laugh.

"Who was she?"

Seated on an old velvet sofa with my feet planted firmly on the floor, I rough my hand down my face and rest my elbows on my knees. "My ex-wife. Fred's daughter."

"You mentioned that, but do you want to talk?"

"No." I never have and I never will, not even with my

closest friends or the guys on the team. However, I did mention it to Book Shop Girl. I'll admit venting brought some relief.

"Whatever happened, I'm sorry. You seem like you would've been a great husband, loving, loyal, and protective."

On a reflexive grunt of acknowledgment, the story tumbles out. "She was what was called a 'Puck bunny,' a team fan, always around, cheering us on. The guys said to stay away from girls like her. I thought Ilyssa was different. She captivated me. Made me feel appreciated, I guess. I don't know. Looking back, it was like I was under a spell. I was at the height of my career and had everything, except honesty, as it turns out. She cheated on me with guys from several rival teams. I felt disgraced."

"Dishonored," Gracie says, eyes filled with sorrow.

I want to tell her not to worry about it. I'm fine. She should go back to living in Smileyville, but given her expression, she feels emotions for me that I haven't allowed myself to experience. My breath stalls.

"I told her it was over three times before she got the message. And I let myself be drawn back in. Each time, I got word that she hooked up with someone else while I was out of town. When I officially filed for divorce, she went from clingy to cold, and that's when the real trouble started."

"That couldn't have been easy."

"Yes and no. The worst part was quitting hockey. I dug into a deep, deep hole. My life was on a swift decline."

"What changed?" The cat curls up on Gracie's lap and purrs.

Talking, er, emailing. I'm not the kind of guy who'd

criticize a dude for crying, but it's not something I do. Maybe I have a sodium deficiency or something. However, chatting with BSG all those months and having an outlet where my life felt normal helped me deal with everything else. I didn't realize it until now. "Someone encouraged me without realizing it. Helped me dig out of the hole I was in. But before that, I became an assistant coach which helped too because the divorce took forever. Just to get out of it, I let Ilyssa have everything."

"But you got her dad's property."

"Is that what they call poetic justice?"

"I think Mr. Foxx was looking out for you. For both of us," she adds softly.

"There are two things in this world I love, and they're the same two things I'm good at: playing and coaching hockey. I'm not a businessman. I figured turning this into a parking lot would make the most sense. I hate fighting to the death for a spot and the idea came to me at the airport when I was trying to return my rental car. I'm big on the follow-through. Come up with a plan, and don't deviate. Then again, I still need to get a new car."

"That's a story you're telling yourself."

"That I need a new car?"

"That there are only two things you're good at. It's a way to play it safe."

"I play and coach hockey. It's a dangerous sport. Nothing safe about it."

"I mean emotionally," she trills as if that should be obvious.

A reflexive grunt escapes. "I'll take that under consideration." But that's just my nice way of shutting down this conversation because it's getting personal, and with that comes far too much risk.

Gracie doesn't press though. Instead, she says, "As for me, I'm a shy book lover who someday wants to get married and have a family."

"Let me guess, you are single because you fall for the wrong kinds of men. The kind who don't want what you do."

"More like I'm holding out hope for the right one. Meg and Kara say my standards are too high. But I've never even been asked out."

I scoff. "I find that hard to believe."

She tries to hide her frown. "If this were the eighties, fine, but things are different now."

"Are you saying I'm old? I'm in my early thirties."

"I'm in my late twenties. But I meant the eighteen-eighties. We live in the modern day."

"There's nothing wrong with old-fashioned romance."

"Says the beast."

I chuckle. "And you're brazen."

"I'm trying to be brave." The cat hops from Gracie's lap and pads over to me.

"You said that you're shy. There's nothing wrong with that, but you're also a ray of sunshine." The comment comes out of my mouth as if it were beamed there from above.

"Tell that to the storm."

The lights flicker.

She shivers. I lift my hand to brush a piece of her hair from her forehead. From the rain, her waves turned into messy curls, but I rather like the wild look. "How's your head?"

"The ice helped. Thanks again."

Her gaze drifts to mine as if she wants to tell me that she appreciates that I care, but is afraid I'll say something snide. She's not wrong. That's been my mood for a while now, but it dissolves, washing away in the weather.

Gracie's eyes are the softest, warmest brown. This could be an intimate moment, but I should shut it down. That's the voice of reason. There's another one inside with a different message.

I'm torn about which one to heed. Semi-recent experience suggests I'm better off being alone. But the reality of the woman in front of me kindles a yearning I only now recognize, but it doesn't come from the same place as what drove me to hook up with Ilyssa, give in to her pressure, and pretend everything was fine. That was me masquerading as the guy I thought I was supposed to be.

With Gracie, the stirrings inside come from deep down, telling me that this is something real. Strange as it sounds, I have to agree, Fred had something to do with this.

Eight

VOHN

GRACIE BOUNCES SLIGHTLY on the sofa and crisscrosses her legs. "If I'm shy sunshine, you're a grumpy cinnamon roll."

I sip from a water bottle and almost do a spit take. "A what?"

"A grumpy cinnamon roll," she repeats.

"Is that like a cinnamon bun?" Nat, the team nutritionist, would have those on the red light food list, meaning we're not indulging.

"In romance, a cinnamon roll character is both buttery and sweet, but it's not always obvious."

"I'm neither of those things. Promise."

"You're certainly not doughy." Her gaze flits to my abs and biceps and then away. "I left out the cinnamon part—they're a bit spicy too. There can be a lot hidden in the cinnamon sugar spiral, but on the outside, you project pure grump, which is just what it sounds like."

"And women like that?"

"Some women do."

The real question is, does she? Am I the type of man Gracie wants? Could I get married again and have a family? I did the first part, but Ilyssa didn't want kids. Wish I'd known that before I caved into the pressure to tie the knot. The stiff control over my life and the boundaries I've put in place since the breakup fades. I give my head a little shake, trying to return to my senses.

Clearing my throat, I say, "I'm more of a puck guy than a cinnamon whatever. Are you hungry? I grabbed a bag of cheesy popcorn, chocolate-coated and peanut butter-filled pretzels, and—" I read a package. "Coco Loco Cocoa bites. It's what I could find."

"Chef's kiss. Those are perfect."

"Lots of packaged foods."

She exaggeratedly recoils. "Are you criticizing my snack options?"

"Not much healthy here."

"Do you have to stick to the team nutritionist's guidelines even though you're a coach? Can't you have whatever you want?"

Her eyes widen, tempting me.

"While that's true, I spend a lot of time training with the guys, so I want to keep in top form."

"You're succeeding," she says, hiding a smirk by popping one of the coconut-chocolate cluster things in her mouth.

There goes that flare again. You'd think it would be out of juice by now much like my phone, sadly I haven't heard from BookshopGirl.

Then my phone pings and I blink a few times, hardly able to believe my eyes.

The subject line is Tornado Warning with a little emoji. Maybe she's been close to me all along. Though, I can't lie, I am conflicted given my attraction to Gracie as much as I try to resist it.

"Why are you smiling?" I ask her, considering everything that just happened.

With a little bobble of her head, she says, "I just emailed my secret book boyfriend to report that I'm safe and sound."

My jaw lowers. "Your what boyfriend?"

"This is a judgment-free zone."

My thoughts slow along with my pulse and I flick to my email app. Sure enough, there's an email from BookShop-Girl. My gaze lifts to Gracie and that first night spills into my mind... How did I not make the connection, considering she owns a bookstore?

A little voice tells me that it's because I was afraid. I knew that if I ever met BSG, I'd be all in, head over heels...er, skates.

"Gracie, have, uh, you been emailing someone?" My mouth is dry like I've been chewing chalk.

She giggles. "Yeah, as I said, my secret book boyfriend. Well, he goes by #33, and at first, he was kind of distant and closed off, but what can you expect? Mr. Foxx did to us what I do with readers and books."

Matchmaker is right.

Her eyes widen slightly as if slowly realizing the same thing as me. "Wait, why do you ask?"

"The last time I saw Fred was when I was deep into the divorce proceedings. He said licking my wounds for too long would make me mean like a wolf. He told me that I'd soon be receiving a unique email and that I should reply. He asked me to, in fact. They came from BookShopGirl, aka BSG."

"No."

"Yes."

"Nooo," she says, lengthening the word.

I nod and turn my phone to face her with the inbox open, showing the email she just sent.

"No way." Gripping my hand and staring into my phone, she studies the message.

My skin burns in the best of ways.

Our gazes float together and then quickly flick apart.

She shakes her head, then nods as if piecing it together.

"I can't believe it either," I say softly because for better or worse, those months of emailing her softened something inside me.

Clearing her throat, as if speaking more to herself than me, Gracie says, "The emails felt old-fashioned minus the paper and pen part. I figured what harm could it do? Mr. Foxx wanted me to write a positive, thoughtful, or sweet note once a month. A few kind words of encouragement. That's all. He said not to share personal details and said to consider it a good deed."

I exhale sharply through my nose. "Great. A charity case."

"At first, I thought that he missed his wife, and this was a way for him to feel connected, young again, and with his whole life and the promise of a relationship ahead. Clearly, it wasn't him. As time passed and I got to know the guy he asked me to email, I figured I was chatting with his bachelor son or single nephew in need of an anonymous friend."

"He said to let the email be a sounding board, an outlet, but more importantly to listen. He warned me not to share any personal information. The guy got more peculiar the longer I knew him, so the email thing didn't strike me as that odd."

She presses her hand to her forehead, thoughts scattering in every direction. "So you're #33?"

"And you're BookShopGirl." My voice sounds distant and hardly like my own.

We stare at each other for a long moment before quickly looking away again.

Opening the container of pretzels, Gracie's voice races when she says, "I feel snacky. Do you get snacky?"

Treating this as if it's one of our emails, I use her language. "More like regrety." A long exhale comes before I confess the truth. "Retiring, amidst all the divorce nonsense, was rough. I didn't get the last game glory that I'd hoped for all of my career. Guess I'm trying to hang onto it however I can. I think Fred noticed and was trying to help."

The difficulty of the last few years had still been gnawing away at me inside, but as soon as the words are out, it splinters apart. Sure, a few pieces remain, but it's no longer a giant painful mass.

Brow knitted with empathy, rather than pity, Gracie grips my pinky and gives it a wiggle. It's a comforting gesture. "I'm guessing the guys on the team appreciate your commitment."

"Always looking on the bright side, huh?"

"It's better than staying in the storm. I hope this one passes quickly without leaving much damage."

The words remind me about the walls I built around

myself and how they could come crumbling down if I let them.

While we eat, I plug in my phone to charge and then give an updated weather report. As soon as I relay that the tornado warning is still in effect, the power goes out.

I flick on the flashlight on my phone so we can finish eating. When we're done, we talk, our voices filling the dark space. We start by discussing Fred, which shifts into our email exchanges. I've been conversing with this woman for months. Strange that we're already acquaintances...friends?

"Funny that you're NumberThirtyThree@email. At first, I couldn't match the messages with your general appearance and demeanor." She waves her hand over my silhouette. "But it makes an unexpected kind of sense now."

"And you're BookShopGirl@email," I say, still hardly able to believe it. And more beautiful and amazing than I could've imagined. "We can blame Fred."

"Or thank him. But does this change things?" She inches closer.

"Do we want it to?" A long-forgotten yearning whispers through me.

Her eyes flirt to mine but don't land on my lips.

I pick up the gold, filigree locket on a chain around her neck. "This looks like a family heirloom."

Gracie's fingers lightly touch mine and my entire body relaxes, like when slipping into a warm bath after a hard workout.

She says, "It was my mother's. She and my dad died in an accident a week after my fifth birthday. My earliest memory is of her reading to me. All the while, I'd open and close the locket. Probably drove her crazy, but she never seemed to mind." She presses the tiny button, and it pops open, revealing two old photographs.

On the left is a small, faded photo of a couple, and on the right is the same couple, though slightly older, with a baby in their arms.

"I take it that's baby Gracie."

She nods. "When I learned to read, my mom and I would take turns reading out of my favorite books, but I never got tired of looking at the locket. Her big dream was to open a bookstore, and my dad was a coffee aficionado. He was going to run a little café out of it. They were on the way to the bank to sign the loan when their car was struck. They didn't make it."

"I am so sorry." My heart aches for her loss.

She nods as if she appreciates the sentiment but still feels the sting, even after all this time. It's only now that behind her sunny smile is a well of sadness, tears that'll never dry up.

"I was sent to live with my uncle who was old and miserable. My life became devoid of touch and laughter. Smiles and simple conversation. Eventually, he sent me to boarding school." Her voice is hollow.

"Despite that, you remained cheerful."

"It was that or turn out like him. I never gave up on wanting a family. Opening the shop was a way to bring them closer to me because not only will I not get mine back, but it doesn't look like I'll ever have one of my own."

"There's still time."

"There are a few steps that would need to happen first.

You're talking to someone who's never been on a date, much less had her first kiss."

"But that's not always the case in books, right?"

"S'pose not. Sometimes it's instalove or love at first sight, and in others falling in love is a slow and painful process."

"And everything in between?" I ask.

Gracie nods. "Speaking of love stories..." She pulls a slim tablet out of her tote bag. When she turns it on, the light illuminates her face with wide eyes fringed by dark lashes. My gaze coasts along the smooth slope of her nose and cheeks which are lifted with a smile before landing on her lips.

Gracie says, "Want to hear the greatest love story of all time?"

"Is that an official superlative?"

"There's no arguing with Pride and Prejudice, by Jane Austen."

Wishing to erase the hurt she carries or at least make her feel lighter, more buoyant, I say, "Not to be confused with Janey Pawsten,"

She giggles. "Author of Purred and Prejudice."

I pet the cat in my lap while Gracie reads to me. I instantly object to Mr. Darcy, but I also kind of relate.

Intermittently, I interrupt, asking questions about why Mrs. Bennet was so intent on marrying off her daughters and how the characters generally came into partnerships of marriage before falling in love.

Gracie's voice is thoughtful when she says, "Some people think it's old-fashioned, but I rather like that the promise to be together comes first. Together, they build toward the happily ever after."

That's definitely not how Ilyssa and I did things, and look how horribly that worked out.

"Do you think those couples ever fall in love?"

"It can take seconds to fall in love, Vohn. The real question is staying in love, but they made a promise to each other and part of that is navigating life's challenges and growing together." She answers with such honesty and sincerity that I do not argue.

Later, I ask whether Gracie would pick Mr. Bingley, Mr. Darcy, or Mr. Wickham for her suitor.

She squawks a laugh. "Isn't it obvious?"

No, but even if it were, I'd want to hear her say it.

"Mr. Darcy, of course."

Pressing her lips together to hide a smile, she continues to read.

About halfway through, I say, "This should be a movie."

"It is. Well, there are about nine screen adaptions, including one with zombies." She wrinkles her nose.

"I take it that's not your favorite."

"Definitely not."

"Which one is?" The more time I spend with her, the more I want to know.

Gracie taps her chin in thought. "The one when they almost kiss in the rain. Although people argue that the scene isn't true to the book. At that point in the story, they're squarely on opposite sides of the enemies-to-lovers spectrum."

"It's not a grumpy sunshine romance?"

She tips her head from side to side. "That can be argued, but I think the enemies-to-lovers trope fits better. He's broody, but she's not super sunny."

But Gracie is.

"Grumpy and broody, huh? Like me."

"Very much so."

I nudge her, and she slides closer on the lumpy sofa.

"Except I'm letting you read to me," I tease.

"What other choice do you have?"

"I could go brood in the corner."

She tosses her head back with laughter, startling Janey who rushes to hide under the chair again.

"Or we could almost kiss in the rain," I suggest.

"Are you saying we go check the weather?"

Wearing a smirk and holding her gaze in the dim light, I shrug. "Here is fine too."

"Oh." The word catches as if she realizes what I mean. She leans in, eyelashes sweeping her cheeks, and then pauses. "I've never done this before."

I'm not sure what to say because it feels like an honor to be her first kiss.

She dips her head and inhales.

I tuck a piece of her hair behind her ear. It's silky soft. "Am I right to assume there's always a first in those romances of yours? First glance, first conversation, first kiss…"

Gentle brown eyes lifting to mine, she doesn't say another word and only nods. The space closes between us and our mouths meet.

The warmth of her lips radiates through me, sending a spiral of something directly to my chest. Before I can question what it is, my mind shuts down as my fingers trail the length of her neck and stop at the locket.

The kiss is slight before we both pull away. More like an almost kiss. Regret fights with the rising heat inside.

She lets out an unsteady breath. "Wow. That escalated quickly."

Yeah. I want more but know better than to give what I don't have—what she deserves. A man with a heart. We're in the eye of the storm down here and will have to return to reality by daybreak. Best not to complicate things.

Sleepily rubbing her eyes, Gracie goes back to reading. Her fingers absently touch her locket and then drift to her lower lip. I'm not sure what time it is when I doze off. But Elizabeth and the Gardiners had just arrived at Pemberley while I reminded myself that I'm the kind of guy who women leave.

Sometime later, I wake up with my arm snugly around Gracie. Curled up on the sofa beside me, the lump on her forehead has gone down, and the cat is cuddled up between us for maximum warmth. If we weren't in the basement, it would be a cozy scene.

I watch over this radiant, unique, and beautiful woman. She's so pure, so innocent. I don't want to ruin her. I wonder how Mr. Darcy resisted for so long.

Curious, I turn on her tablet and read until I reach the epilogue, leaving me to ask myself what I believe. Does love conquer all?

After a few hours of rest, I wake up to my phone buzzing with a text. Gracie's head rests on my shoulder. Her full lips lift in the slightest smile, and her lilac almond scent makes me want to stay here forever. Well, not the basement, but with her in a fictional oasis where hearts don't get crushed and lives practically destroyed.

I reluctantly and carefully extract myself from the squeaky old velvet sofa. The text message is from Badaszek writing that the weather cleared up and we have ice time at seven sharp.

That's in an hour.

Gracie, probably having sweet dreams of cinnamon rolls and happily ever afters, deserves so much more than anything I could ever give her.

As I quietly walk upstairs and out of her life—except to make sure she clears out of the bookstore—my phone rings. I answer it, thinking it's the coach, and say, "I'll be there, and whatever you heard about me rescuing a damsel in distress, it's not true."

A different voice than the one I expect replies. "Vohn? This is Eric Simons, the team lawyer. I'm calling about your work visa. We have a problem."

I definitely do. It's that only thirty seconds have passed since I've been away from Gracie, and my heart feels like it's cooling over, like a Zamboni resurfacing the ice.

Nine

GRACIE

SQUINTING against the gray overcast sky, I feel like a mole person as I emerge from the musty basement the next morning. The storm left behind a wind-blown mess in the street...and in my mind.

What happened last night? As I settle Janey in upstairs and freshen up, I recount every moment since the last time I was in the bookstore.

When I flip the sign to open, I catalog what I lost:

- My clear bubble umbrella
- My cat, almost
- Potentially my store

What I found:

- That Vohn isn't pure beast—there's some tenderness there
- His lips are what I've been missing from my life

- The basement isn't so bad and just needs a thorough cleaning and fresh paint on the cinderblocks

As for the damage outside, it's minimal, though Kara texts to say the roof of her old Dodge has three golf ball-sized dents. Meg lost a branch off of her beloved Japanese lilac tree that was just about to bloom.

I tell them about getting bonked in the head. They're both incredibly concerned and arrive promptly with coffee and cornbread doughnuts courtesy of the Busy Bee, the bakery down the street. Their specialty is all things corn and honey-related, including honey-infused lattes, my go-to beverage.

"You should see Hatley Street. Mr. Kingston's shed is on the sidewalk. The Logrono's kiddie pool floated clear to the end and is dammed up along with Maureen and Scott Nelson's patio furniture. It's a mess," Kara reports.

"Molly has an assortment of hailstones in the freezer. When things calmed down, she collected them from the porch. The biggest one is the size of a baseball." Meg demonstrates the circumference with her hands.

"Don't tell me that's what hit you on the head." Kara rubs hers.

I share the details of Janey escaping and some of what happened next.

"The book would be called *A Tale of a True Cat Mom*." Meg swipes her hands with a flourish as if presenting the title to an editor.

"*And the Beast who Rescued them Both*," Kara adds.

They burst into laughter.

For some reason, my cheeks flush. "How'd you know that Vohn and I—?"

"Everyone knows you hunkered down with Vohn Brandt. It's the talk of the town," Kara says.

Meg eyes my forehead. "Looks like he took good care of you."

"I wouldn't have pegged him for the caring sort," Kara says.

I fixate on the last doughnut as we fall into a hush that feels loaded with everything I haven't shared with them about last night. I give in, helping myself to the rest of the doughnut. My blazing cheeks betray me.

"Wait," Meg whispers.

"Oh. My. Goodness," Kara says, picking up on Meg's meaning. "You kissed? This is epic."

Meg says, "You don't have to kiss and tell, Gracie."

I love words, they're a big part of my life, but I'm not sure I have the right ones to recount the kiss that sent feverish tingles over every inch of my body and how my stomach fluttered like the winds from an F5 tornado.

Thankfully, Professor Kara doesn't pause for me to share the specifics and launches into a Vohn Brandt 101 lesson. "In the hockey world, he was king for several years. All the women were clamoring for him. He started with Arizona and played briefly for the Wisconsin Warriors before settling here with the Knights. He was an avid dater and the puck bunnies created a bracket, like in basketball, to see who'd win him."

Meg nods. "For a time, Vohn was the player prince of the NHL."

"Player as in lots of girlfriends," Kara clarifies.

"Until Ilyssa got her claws into him," Meg says with disgust.

"I take it you were not a fan," I say, dabbing a crumb with my pointer finger and wishing there were more doughnuts.

Meg and Kara shake their heads, making stink faces.

"All the guys thought she was cute, but her personality was the pits," Kara says.

"She was cunning," Meg adds.

"Manipulative."

"Mean."

Kara eyes Meg, and she gives a slight nod. "For example, two weeks after Meg and Micah got married, Ilyssa cornered him outside the locker room and tried to smooch him. He did everything he could to stave her off. It was all caught on the security footage."

"Why would Vohn marry someone like that?" I ask more to myself than them.

"I'd argue he gave into her demands. Also, the Knights are super family-oriented, more so than the other teams. Coach Badaszek encourages real, lasting relationships rather than flavors of the week. He says it makes the guys more focused and demonstrates commitment. He has a whole speech he gives to new players, so it could have had something to do with that," Meg explains.

"Or it could've been blackmail. Just saying," Kara adds.

Meg shakes her head. "He had nothing to hide. She's the one who cheated on him."

"And yet she made their divorce ugly and public."

"Him giving into her for marriage fits since he said that he let her have everything in the divorce—their house, car, and all that," I say, but the guy is anything but a pushover. I'd defy the tornado winds to knock him down.

"He lost everything, including his smile," Meg says. "It was a fan favorite."

"She turned him into a beast."

I let out a sigh because last night I glimpsed who he may have once been, who he could become.

Meg bounces on her toes and imitates my sigh. "I know that sound. So you find him attractive?"

"Do you need to ask?" Kara fans herself as if his hotness is obvious.

To me, too. "He's taller than me." This is a plus, but I don't say the part about how his stormy eyes settled in the moments before his mouth landed on mine, or how the corners of his lips lift ever so slightly while I'm talking, and the dimple in his chin is adorable. I mean, adorably manly.

"We had such a good conversation, much like in our emails. It's like we both forgot about the whole breaking and entering debacle."

"Emails?" Kara asks, perceptive.

I tell them all about Mr. Foxx and the messages.

"He was your book boyfriend?" Meg asks, shocked. "This. Is. Wild."

"So Vohn listening to you was the best part?" Kara waggles her eyebrows.

I bite my lip and glance away...and the kiss.

"On a romance scale of one to ten, with one being a squid and ten being a spicy hot pepper, how was the kiss?" she asks.

Before I can answer or confess that I don't have anything to compare the kiss to since Vohn was my first, a few students come in; apparently, school was delayed during hail storm clean-up efforts.

"We'll get it out of you later," Kara says.

They both wave goodbye. The rest of the morning is relatively busy, and I barely have time for lunch. After being sequestered at home for the night, people are out and about, eager to get fresh air and socialize.

I sell copies of the entire Jane Austen catalog to different customers, along with matching seven others to some of my favorite indie romances, plus one that's a rom-com paranormal romance mashup.

Later that afternoon, during a quiet spell, I go to the mini fridge in the storage room at the back of the store when the door jingles.

Vohn stands in the entry, backlit by the gray sky. He's a broad-shouldered silhouette with his hands on his hips and his stance wide. For a second, I imagine he's here to sweep me off my feet and kiss me, but I should know better.

Vohn already told me he's going to do the opposite. He's here to sweep me and my bookstore to the curb.

Ten

GRACIE

I'M NOT sure what last night meant for Vohn and me, but I'm not giving up on convincing him to let me keep the store open.

I didn't tell Meg and Kara about his threat because, although I adore them, word would spread invisibly like the wind. I don't want to hear even a whiff of gossip before I exhaust my attempts to keep my dream alive.

Stepping into full view, I say, "Welcome to Once Upon a Romance. Can I interest you in some chocolate milk?"

Given the fact Vohn said he was kicking me out the last time he walked into my store, I shouldn't even let him in, but I'm not giving up hope that he'll change his mind.

"What am I, eight?" He steps closer, looming over me.

Yet his lingering gaze never wavers from following my every movement. It's not creepy in an Edward Cullen watching Bella sleep kind of way. More like he's admiring me. For so long, I've been self-conscious about my height, but Vohn, despite our rough start, makes me feel confident and like I can stand tall, stand up to him.

"Doesn't everyone have afternoon chocolate milk?" I lean in. "But so you know, I only offer it to special customers."

His expression wavers as if he's thinking about last night or he's not sure what to make of me. I can't tell.

With a singsong voice, I say, "I use the finest Brazilian cocoa."

"You would, huh? You certainly don't seem like a person who would use chocolate syrup from a squeeze bottle."

Feeling called out, I own my chocolate addiction. "Oh, I do, but that's reserved for late-night cravings when I drizzle it directly in my mouth." I tip my head back and demonstrate. I'll have to add that to my grocery list when my budget allows.

Vohn's gaze lands on my lips, and he licks his. Our gazes catch and hold for one long heart-pounding moment.

My cheeks feel warm again when I realize how my comment sounded, like it was straight out of a romance novel. "I appreciate a square of the finest specialty chocolate in the world and won't say no to a foil-wrapped chocolate kiss candy either. I'd like to make it known that I'm not a chocolate snob."

"I'll remember that on Valentine's Day." Vohn's lips quirk and something plays in his eyes—amusement, desire, yearning?

"I wouldn't expect a guy like you to entertain Valentine's Day."

"We all have our weaknesses."

Are we...flirting? Or is Vohn referring to his weakness in giving in to Ilyssa?

"Yeah, I'll take the chocolate milk," he says, sitting down on the metal chair by the bistro table.

When it warms up later in the spring and the threat of storms has passed, I'll put the table outside and serve chocolate milk. Lemonade. Coffee and tea for sure. First, I'll have to make more room in the back and have a sink installed.

But I'm getting ahead of myself. Vohn is here to tell me that the bookstore has to close. My abrupt movement makes a few drops of my chocolate milk spill onto my hand. I lick it off and turn slightly to make sure he didn't notice.

But Vohn stares at me intently. Eyes heavy and lips parted slightly, he wears what could best be described as a smolder.

My throat bobs with a swallow as I set down his glass on the table. He takes a long drink and says, "Haven't had this in years."

Never before have I wished that I were a glass of chocolate milk, yet here we are. Clearing my throat, I say, "You're welcome. It might help you not to hate fun so much."

"Who said I hated fun?"

"You said yourself that you hadn't had a glass of chocolate milk in a long time. Drinking chocolate milk is fun."

He lets out a sound that could be a chuckle if the man didn't eat rocks and ice for breakfast. "There are a lot of other fun things that I do."

"I'm not convinced. Name one," I challenge.

"Play hockey."

"Name another."

He stammers and says, "Skate."

"Is that what you were doing this morning?"

"And thinking..."

"How human of you," I say because he gives off major beast vibes and I'm not letting down my guard while I live in fear that he's kicking me out of my store.

Getting to his feet, Vohn folds his arms in front of his chest and paces as if he needs the motion to get the words out. "I've always believed that hockey is it for me. I'm lousy at relationships. I have no idea how to be a landlord. There's just hockey. But maybe I want more."

"Nothing wrong with that."

He goes still for a long moment and then drops to sitting as if he needs the chair while delivering this information. "There has been a change of plans."

I brace myself for the worst. Not only is he going to bulldoze the store, but the wrecking ball is here right now. "Please let me box up some of my beloved books first."

Vohn grabs my wrist, stopping me. I practically fall into his lap.

He says, "I need you to listen to me. This is serious. I was born in Germany. Moved here when I was seventeen to play hockey. I was on a work visa, and a dirty, tricky loophole during the divorce recently came to my lawyer's attention. If I don't remarry, not only will I be deported, I'll lose this property."

My sweet romantic heart falls. "Is that why you gave in and married Ilyssa in the first place?"

"So I could get my citizenship? No. I almost wish that were the case because—" He looks at the floor and an uncharacteristically sad expression flits across his face. "I wasn't perfect by any means, but I tried. Gave her the best of me. Now, all that's left is—never mind. We don't need to talk about that."

"You're not as much of a beast as I thought. I think there's still some of that goodness left. I'm sorry about the citizenship trouble. Does this mean you're going to sell the building? If I could afford to buy it from you, I would." It's selfish, given the trouble Vohn faces, but hope wells inside because maybe whoever buys it will let me remain open.

"No, I lose it to Ilyssa. She's Fred's next of kin."

"Maybe if I talk to her—"

"Gracie, she's not like you. Her definition of fun is making kids cry."

My eyes bulge. "Is she that bad?"

"I mean, when they see her, they're terrified. After all the plastic surgery she's had, she looks like a creature conjured from nightmares. I'm not saying this to be rude. It's true."

"Kara and Meg said she used to be pretty, but..." I go quiet, not wanting to gossip.

Vohn still holds my wrist. My skin is hot where we touch. His palm drops to my hand and he holds it.

Glancing at our hands and how his closes so fully over mine, wrapping it in a snug blanket, I say, "I wish I could help."

"You'd help me even though I said I was going to level this building, forcing you to close your shop?"

My shoulder lifts with a shrug. "I'm not a pushover. More like I don't wish ill on you. And maybe if I show you kindness you'll return the favor. A good deed, a pay it forward kind of thing like Mr. Foxx said."

With a decisive nod, Vohn says, "I will. To get me out of this fix, I'd like to propose a fake marriage."

My smile slips, and I draw back, understanding what

he's saying in the context of romance novels but not as it applies to real life.

He reaches for my hand, and hope rises inside, but then I remember the cardinal rule of the marriage of convenience trope. It's fake.

...Well, until it's not.

Eleven

VOHN

I CANNOT BELIEVE the words that came out of my mouth. It's entirely irrational and probably illegal, but I said what I said.

Maybe marriage could work for us and fix my citizenship situation, and maybe it would turn into something more. But that's more of an afterthought as I watch Gracie process the situation.

A line etches itself between her brows, and her eyes dart around the room as if looking for an escape route. "You're joking."

I shove my hands in my pockets, second-guessing myself. Maybe it's being surrounded by stories and romance or having just chugged down a glass of chocolate milk, but the idea materialized, and I ran with it, like I would when streaking down the rink toward the goal.

In hockey, once you commit, it's all or nothing. Sudden death.

Trepidation fills Gracie's voice when she asks, "So you want to marry me?"

Unsure whether she's all in or ready to run for the hills, I pivot. My reply is part question, part statement. "Temporarily, if you want. No pressure."

Her first two fingers brush her bottom lip, and she paces slowly. "But I only just had my first kiss."

My jaw lowers. "So you weren't kidding. Last night was your first kiss?"

She nods.

"With me?" I choke out, grasping the meaning of it.

I'm not comparing Gracie to Ilyssa, but it's hard not to notice the stark contrast. Ilyssa literally had a list of every hockey player in the NHL who was single. She'd crossed off over a hundred of them because they'd kissed.

Whether Gracie never had the opportunity or had waited, I was her first. Me. Not to sound conceited, but it was a great kiss, even if it was far too brief.

"I told you that I had never been asked out. Haven't even been on a first date. Isn't this jumping in fast?"

Yes, but she's my only hope...and my heart does a strange thing around Gracie that makes me want more—more time with her, more listening to her, more getting to know her.

But so she doesn't spook, I'm quick to remind Gracie that it doesn't have to be real. "Just for a matter of convenience."

Her expression flickers.

"Think of me as one of the heroes from a book. Mr. Darcy or whoever."

"But he really, truly loved Elizabeth."

That throbbing thing in my chest practically tries to

punch its way out. I press my hand there. "Well, um, he didn't realize it right away. He was clouded by his pride."

"You've got that right. He was also aloof, self-important, and rude," she replies.

"Elizabeth despised him at first, too. But you could argue that there was an initial attraction sparking between them at the ball in Meryton."

"They had a terrible first impression. He said she was tolerable but not tempting. Not handsome." Gracie frowns.

"I should hope not," I say.

Gracie gasps. "But Elizabeth overheard him saying that about *her*. He rejected Elizabeth."

My eyebrow lifts, and then I capture Gracie's gaze. "Mr. Darcy never said she wasn't beautiful."

She sucks in a breath as if realizing the distinction. "Yet he did everything he could to push her away."

I reach for Gracie, clasping her upper arms. "But if you skip to the good part, he eventually expresses his admiration and love for her."

"He said she bewitched him. That sounds a lot like something Ilyssa would do."

I snort. "No, Ilyssa was nothing like Elizabeth. What we had wasn't love. Darcy only came to know what that felt like when he was in the middle of it." I almost stagger because I relate so deeply, so fully.

"Does that mean you finished reading Pride and Prejudice?"

"I haven't quite gotten to the happily ever after. But yes, I stayed up last night, keeping watch, making sure you were okay, and I couldn't put it down," I admit.

Gracie's jaw works like she wants to defy me or protest. Instead, she dabs her forehead. "Thank you. The lump is hardly there."

"Will you do it?" I ask.

She sinks back. "Will I marry you for convenience? What's in it for me?"

"I thought that was obvious." My gaze slides to the nearest bookshelf, and I nod.

Leaping up and down, Gracie bunches her hands under her chin. "You mean I don't have to close the store? I'm so relieved. Excited. Really?"

I nod, and she throws her arms around me, squeezing tight. "Yay. Thank you."

Relief comes close to me too, but something else stops it from sweeping through me entirely. I'm asking a woman who loves romance to marry me under false pretenses, but it's not like I kept that from her. The fake part is no secret, so should it matter?

Do I want it to be something else? I'm afraid to answer that question.

I blurt, "So you'll do it?"

She goes still as if having the same thought, wondering where reality ends and fiction begins. "Um, well, that's not exactly the future I'd hoped for."

"But you said you wanted to get married."

"For real. For love." Gracie's voice is small.

"Didn't they have arranged marriages during the olden days? Mrs. Bennet was obsessed with marrying off her daughters for practical, financial, and security reasons."

"I suppose so, but..."

I want to tell her that we can divorce as soon as possible

so she can find her Prince Charming. The words trip on my tongue because maybe this is how things will start, but the story wink will lead to a beginning, not an end. "Consult your novels. Do things usually work out for the main characters?"

Her brown eyes fill with hope. "Do you want things to?"

The question she's really asking shifts into focus, and I do my best to speed skate away from it.

"I don't want to lose," I clear my throat, "my job."

But if the next fifty years are anything like last night, I do not object.

"I need time to think. This is happening fast."

"I understand." Hand on the doorknob, I paraphrase something Elizabeth said about herself and Mr. Darcy never being able to make each other happy. But then I add a variation of what he said to her later, "But maybe I could love you most ardently."

I'm halfway out the door when Gracie rushes over to me, her skirt swishing around her legs. "Do you believe you're worthy of love?"

I'm slow to tell the truth. "I didn't for a long time."

As if measuring my response against the complicated system she has for matching readers with the perfect story, she asks, "Do you think love at first sight is possible?"

Nodding, I answer, "And love after a first kiss."

I grip her jaw in my closed hand and rub my thumb along her cheek.

"Does that mean—?"

"Ever since we met, I see evidence of you everywhere. I didn't want anything to do with it, but I cannot avoid whatever is happening between us. I'm not sure what it means other than I don't despise you, which must mean I—"

Lifting onto her toes, she says, "Let's double-check to be sure."

Surrounded by books and stories, the only one that matters right now is the true one that I tell myself. This woman has broken through the wall around my chest. Slowly over the last nine months through our emails, she's brought sweetness back into my life. Then very quickly, she made it stick. But she hasn't tricked me or manipulated me. No, this is real.

Anticipation coils inside as we tip closer, leaving questions behind and leaning into certainty, commitment, and our story.

For the first time in a long time, I smile and melt into Gracie's lips.

Twelve

∞

GRACIE

THE FIRST TIME Vohn and I kissed, all I could think about was, *What if I don't know how to do this?* Reading kissing scenes isn't the same as actually kissing.

But I abandon all my thoughts and let his mouth claim mine. Even if I don't know what to do, he does, and that's more than enough.

He stills the trembling inside that's so often caused me to feel insecure for being so tall. The lack of touch and affection after I lost my parents, made me believe I wasn't good enough for anyone. Unlovable. But Vohn's hands and attentiveness say otherwise.

Flutters and tingles spiral and swirl inside as his lips press to mine. It starts as a brush, just as before, but soon we both commit to the kiss, our mouths firmly together.

Vohn's hands thread through my hair, and my palms splay on his strong back. His chest rises and falls with the beat of his heart. My pulse pounds as my breath comes rapidly.

Curling into the kiss, my body, heart, and mind crave

more of this. How have I been missing this all my life? But I am so glad I waited.

My hands skim his shoulders, smoothing their way to his neck, before landing just below his ears, cupping the edge of his jaw. I've hardly experienced this kind of touch, and having free access to his skin, stubble, and strong muscles is like the summer sun after a lifetime of winters.

Meanwhile, Vohn's fingers rove and explore, brushing my collarbones before his hands smooth down my arms and he wraps me up, snugging me closer.

The deepening kiss tells me that if Vohn ever yearned for anything, he's finally found it. We're tangled in each other, and I give back with all I have. This is better than fiction.

Vohn slowly kisses a trail from my lips to the space by my ear and then along my collarbones. His fingers brush my locket. His attention to it is unexpectedly sweet even though the reason I wear it is bitter.

His eyes find mine as they slowly open, resurfacing. My thoughts return one by one, clicking slowly into place. He asked me to marry him for his green card. Not for real. But was the kiss?

The intensity in his eyes is an affirmation, a promise. But doubt tries to curl around me like smoke. I convince myself that even if it's fake, it could become real.

Straightening, his voice is rough when he says, "I'll be back."

I'm left rosy-cheeked and in shock because I did not see this plot twist coming. Not only do I not have to close Once Upon a Romance, but Vohn read my favorite book of all time, and he gets it. Does that mean he gets me?

As the next hours pass, I close the shop for the day. When he doesn't return, the doubts raise a ruckus. There I was, wearing my romance-colored glasses when in reality this marriage of convenience is a fake relationship.

Vohn needs my help, and I need his. End of story.

But he did paraphrase Darcy. He also said he didn't despise me and that he could learn to love me. Am I being naïve? Falling for this beast of a man?

But maybe like in love stories, since he was my first kiss, he'll turn into a prince.

My laptop pings with a message. It's from Number-ThirtyThree@email.com telling me to be ready at six. Hope bursts through the doubt with a fist lifted in triumph. Before I respond, my phone dings with a text.

> Kara: Why was Vohn Brandt seen at Radiance and Filigree Fine Jewelry?

> Meg: I heard the windows at Once Upon a Romance got steamy today.

I fight the urge to deny and defend myself, but there is no secret keeping in Cobbiton. Between Mrs. Gormely and Kara, a woman can't kiss her book boyfriend in peace. A little smile peeks onto my lips, somehow still warm from earlier.

Then I remind myself it's fake.

> Meg: Juliette from l'Occasion Cobbiton just reported that he made a reservation tonight.

Kara: Ooh la la. Fancy. Do you like French food?

Never mind. Meg is on the gossip list too along with the rest of the town. I fret about how fast this is happening, what's real, and what's for show. I've read a few books where one of the characters needs a green card so they orchestrate a believable love affair. Of course, by the end, they realize their true feelings, but what if we don't? What if I'm being Ilyssa-ed?

Double never mind. I don't want to be cynical, jaded, or unsure. Discouragement isn't what brought me here. Janey rubs her head against my leg, reminding me not to be prideful or prejudiced either.

Two knocks come from the door at the end of the stairwell along with low chatter. It's Meg and Kara, arms full of bags.

"What is going on? Dish it up," says the latter, shoving a shopping bag filled with clothes into my arms.

"Only if you want to, but we're here to help," Meg adds, setting down several garment bags.

I turn in a circle, flustered. "I don't know. Vohn and I kissed last night and spent hours talking and reading. Well, I read to him after the power went out."

"That's so nerdy," Kara says.

"It's also so sweet and so you."

"Then today he came by—" I halt mid-sentence because I probably shouldn't divulge the visa situation. "And we kissed again."

"This is the real-life version of the bonus book we read for the Cover to Cover book club last month," Kara says.

"The instalove romcom?" Meg asks.

"Yes, but this is real life."

"And it seems someone has real feelings for you."

My shoulder lifts shyly. "There's some charm hidden under the gruff and broody demeanor."

Kara snaps her fingers. "I knew you caught feelings for each other."

But they don't know the whole story about the mutually beneficial agreement to save Vohn's citizenship and my shop. All the same, I let them fuss, getting me ready.

"We know all about your book boyfriend wish list."

"What do you mean? I don't have..." I totally do.

"Anytime we read a book, we watch you fall in love with the main character," Meg says sweetly.

It's true.

"And maybe you don't have an actual wish list, but we know if you could write your own male MC, he would be taller than you, strong, and confident."

"Maybe a little rough around the edges."

"Secretly sweet. Outwardly honest and loyal and protective."

"Oh, and affectionate."

Kara wiggles her eyebrows and singsongs, "I think you found someone who checks off those boxes."

I cannot hide my smile. "It's not like I was looking or anything."

Then the three of us jump up and down squealing like we're sixteen and Vohn is my first boyfriend because, well, he is. Thankfully, I don't have downstairs neighbors.

We agree on me wearing a flattering pink dress with my

hair in loose waves. Meg lends me one of her purses, and I wear a sparkly pair of Kara's dangly earrings.

After a glimpse in the mirror, a little sigh escapes.

"She feels it too," Meg says.

"It's spring, and love is in the air," Kara adds.

After thanking them both, I make them leave five minutes before Vohn is supposed to pick me up so my cheeks can return to their natural color and not match my dress.

He arrives in a sleek black Mercedes wearing a pair of slacks, a button-down shirt, and a blazer. Producing a bouquet of gerbera daisies, he says, "For you."

"My favorite, You remembered?"

His lips quirk.

While I'm thinking about how sweet this is, Vohn's voice floats to me as his hand wraps around mine, drawing me closer.

His eyes rove over me as if not sure where to settle. "You look beautiful."

I recall what he said about how Mr. Darcy never said Elizabeth wasn't beautiful...and the way he noticed it in the story...and how he looked at me when he originally spoke those words.

"Thank you, and you look handsome enough to tempt me," I say, reversing what Mr. Darcy said to Elizabeth.

The corners of his lips curl toward a smile as he opens the car's door. "I got my act together today. Finally bought a car...and a truck."

"That was fast."

"My life had all but crept to a halt. Figured it was time to speed things up."

"I imagine giving Ilyssa everything was hard, but starting over is better."

He frowns. "Earlier, I told myself to forget about all that. Start fresh. Clean slate."

While that's encouraging, I pay attention to words—it comes with the book-loving territory—and my hope craters. "Haha. I see what you did there. You got your *act* together. We can't forget this is fake."

Vohn's head snaps in my direction. "Is it?"

"You did propose a fake relationship resulting in a marriage of convenience for your visa, so..."

"It doesn't have to be. The kiss wasn't fake."

The way I feel isn't either, but worry tries to steal my hope like a burglar at the door.

"But the clean slate is only because of the past. Had I not been with Ilyssa, her father wouldn't have left me the property. Take a step or two back, and he wouldn't have asked you to email me."

"I see where you're going with this."

"It was a winding and difficult road of a failed marriage for me—"

"And lonely years of singlehood for me," I finish.

What Meg, Kara, and I were talking about earlier floats into my mind. There's no set pace for love to grow between two people. Trees take years to go from acorn to oak while bamboo is one of the fastest to stretch toward the sun. Both are strong and resilient and long lasting.

Maybe this is real after all.

"I took some time to think earlier. Do it best on the ice. It was then I pivoted. Realized that I was rushing the puck to the wrong goal and about to ruin both our lives. I don't want a parking lot. I want a little bookshop. I want you."

He picks up my hand and kisses my knuckles. A warm pulse rushes through me.

If that wishlist were real, Vohn just added a few more entries. Suddenly shy, even though this is what I've always wanted, I'm not sure what to say so I tell him that.

"You don't have to say anything. All I'd like is a chance," he answers.

Feeling brave, I lean across the center console and kiss him on the cheek. It's an expression of my appreciation and affection. I also want to see his response. Vohn is not the kind of person who is easy to smile, but he wears one now. His eyes sparkle too, and I know for sure that he's my guy.

We drive across town to l'Occasion Cobbiton—an upscale French and Midwest fusion restaurant where Vohn opens the door for me, a perfect gentleman. His palm drops to my lower back when the host leads us to a table for two. A delightful shiver runs along my spine. We browse the menu and chat, picking up where we left off earlier, last night, in our email exchange. It all feels very natural.

"Let me guess, you're going to order the grilled cheese," he says, remembering from our emails.

I nod, using the official menu item name, which is a variation on the classic. "The croque monsieur sandwich. And sources say you're going to get the ribs."

"Ding, ding, ding. You got it."

The server appears, and I place my order. Vohn follows with, "I'll take the cassoulet short ribs, please." A slow smile appears across his lips when she leaves.

"Care to share why the sudden and rare appearance of your smile? I'm suspicious."

"I've come undone. Before I did things because I felt like I had to, otherwise I'd upset, ahem, certain people and have to deal with the fallout. With you, I'm doing this because I want to."

"What prompted this sudden change?"

"The first time I spoke with my lawyer to start the divorce process all those years ago, I stopped living. The call I recently received from the lawyer was a jumpstart. I'd slowed to a crawl except for hockey until you blew in."

"You're the one who broke into my apartment."

He chuckles. "You mean my building?"

"We've only known each other for a short time."

"Is that true, bookshop girl?"

I fiddle with the napkin in my lap. "The truth is I'd been falling for you for a while. You were my secret book boyfriend—a guy I met via email who I wanted to be the lead in my love story."

"Maybe it doesn't need to be a secret anymore. While we might seem like a new couple, we do have a certain comfort level with each other, after last night and months spent emailing."

"Funny, we're on the same page."

For the first time, he chuckles at my joke.

We taste each other's entrees and order dessert, deciding to share. When the crème brûlée arrives, my heart leaps because something gleams in the center, but I realize it's only a little edible decorative gold leaf curl.

We dig in and chat, but when the server brings the

check folder, it's bigger than expected and wrapped in paper.

"I was getting worried." Vohn's smile is tight before he turns to me.

The server winks and whisks away.

My brow furrows with confusion and curiosity.

He clutches the flat, rectangular wrapped package. "You're right, Gracie. This is all happening fast. I woke up yesterday with a dark vision of my future. An empty parking lot of a life. Then the news I got this morning made me realize what's important, what I could lose, but more importantly, what we could gain."

I went from imploding yesterday to seeing a bright future with this man. It chases away my near-constant companion of loneliness, leaving me with a very full heart.

"During our time spent emailing each other, I felt sparks between us. With every exchange, I experienced a yearning for what I imagined I could never have." Vohn smiles with his eyes.

The dread always associated with my loneliness lifts. "We have Mr. Foxx to thank for that."

The corner of his mouth lifts into a smile. "I've never felt this way. Then again, until recently I'd never seen your sunny smile, gorgeous eyes, hopeful outlook, and genuine personality. You're also smart, curious, and thoughtful. You make me want to truly love again and be the best version of myself."

"So you don't hate books?" I ask.

"Or cats or fun or you." Finally, he beams a full smile, and it's like the sun parting the clouds.

I laugh. "Turns out we have a lot in common."

"How do you feel about hockey?"

"I've never been to a game."

"We'll have to change that. Remember when I told you that there are two things in this world that I love and two things that I'm good at?"

"Hockey and hockey."

Catching my gaze and holding it like something precious, he says, "There are three things I love and one of them is at the top of my list. I love you, Gracie."

My racing heart slows and settles, finally having found what I've sought for so long. Vohn's words wrap me in a hug, and it's one I give back. "When I said that I didn't despise you before we kissed in the bookstore, I was kind of thinking the same thing. But this is so irrational. We only just met, apart from emailing."

"Wouldn't your novels tell you that love doesn't always follow a plan?"

"Love cannot be tamed." But his stormy eyes are calm.

He tamed himself for me.

"Seeing as you called me a beast man, I want to prove to you that I can be less of a brute, mostly. I take zero responsibility for my behavior when on the ice. But between you and me...the emails were something I didn't know I needed. I'll admit they lowered my defenses. Made me feel like I had a friend when everything else in my life was uncertain and upside down. Now, meeting you, changes everything."

"Everything?" My hope and anticipation rises like the sun over the horizon with the promise of sunshine and little birds chirping and a bright future.

He nods. "Everything. Gracie Elizabeth, can I ask you a question?"

"How'd you know my middle name?"

His lips quirk. "The building lease."

I gasp, realizing something about our names and the characters in Pride and Prejudice. "Your middle name is Fitz. Like Fitzwilliam Darcy. I saw it on your license. And yes, ask away," I say, letting myself get totally swept away in the moment.

"Maybe it was meant to be." Wearing a boyish smile, Vohn gets to his feet, adjusts his jacket, and then kneels on one knee in front of me.

Everything in the restaurant except for the tinkling music in the background goes quiet. I hold my breath.

Vohn produces a velvet box. Opening it, he asks, "Will you do me the honor of being my real-life book girlfriend wife."

I tip my head back and laugh. "Which one is it?"

"All of the above. Will you marry me, Gracie?" Vohn asks, eyes intent and joking aside.

"Yes, yes, I will."

The room, filled with customers, erupts into claps and cheers. He slides the elegant vintage-style gold ring with fili-gree scrolling around a marquis diamond onto my finger and rises to his feet. It almost matches my locket. His cedar scent envelops me as his arms hold me close and we kiss.

Pardon me while I swoon because nothing feels fake about his hands on my waist, his mouth on mine, or the longing for more—for forever.

"Are we going to do this?" I ask with a hush.

"So long as it's for the right reasons. Not for my visa. For life."

"But do you think we're moving too fast?" I ask one last time just to be sure.

"I set records for speed on the ice, and I feel like I've been waiting all of these years for you."

"Likewise," I say, looking from him to my hand and back again.

We sit down at the table, and Vohn passes me the parcel the server brought over. "A gift for us."

I carefully untie the red ribbon and remove the paper. Inside is a leather-bound book with embossing on the front with the words *Once Upon a Romance* and beneath that it says *Gracie and Vohn Brandt's Love Story.*

He says, "I was hoping you'd say yes."

The giddiness inside makes me bounce in my seat. The flickers and flutters of excitement are better than sweets and books and dreams. The man seated across from me, holding my hand, the ring sparkling between us, and the sincere warmth in his eyes tell me everything I need to know.

"I'll say it now and again every day. I promise to be a good, true, loving, and loyal husband to you for as long as you will have me."

"Spoken like a true Mr. Darcy."

We lean together and kiss, the start of what will become many, many, many more with my not-so-secret book boyfriend.

Epilogue

FIVE YEARS Later

From < BookShopGirl@email.com >
To: < NumberThirtyThree@email.com >
Date: April 10, 10:51 PM
Subject: Out of Office

Hi! I don't dare make a peep because the house is finally quiet. But I have an important question.

Did you put one of those, you know, um, "things" for tomorrow after church under the pail in the backyard? A certain someone named Lizzy has been poking around over there. She's convinced that's where the Easter bunny lives. At our house! Imagine that.

Oh, and I secured the fence around the pool. Freddy was so worried the bunny would fall in. These kids, I tell you.

Thank you for reading them the Easter story board-book before bed. I was falling asleep after our fifth read-through. You're the best. I'm so lucky to call you my secret book boyfriend husband.

Love,

BSG

P.S. I'm having a craving...

~

From < NumberThirtyThree@email.com >
To: < BookShopGirl@email.com >
Date: April 10, 10:53 PM
Re: Out of Office

Hello! I never fail to find the lengths we'll go not to wake the kids up amusing. Funny that you're sitting on the sofa only two inches away. Squeeze my hand when you read this part, and I'll give you a silent kiss. Ha ha.

Never thought on our wedding day that this would be our life. I wouldn't trade it for the world, especially since Freddy is going to someday get the Stanley Cup. Mark my words! And Lizzy loves books just as much as her mom. We have a family legacy going on.

Yes, I put one of the "things" under the pail. Also, by the ladder. Don't want to forget about it since that one is a little out of the way. There are a total of thirty, so we'll have to take a count. We don't want to invite a raccoon into the yard to feast on jelly beans and chocolate eggs.

I happen to love the Easter story, so reading it another five times was no big deal. And I happen to love you so sit tight, and I'll bring you and baby-in-your-belly number three that waffle cone bowl with rainbow sprinkles so long as I can have a bite too.

I love you!

#33

P.S. What do you think about naming the new baby Janey if it's a girl? The cat won't mind. And Austen if it's a boy. I rather like that one.

Thank you for reading! I hope you enjoyed this standalone second-chance romance. I write love stories (*I really wanted to use the word romance here again, but my editing mind won't let me repeat it) with a focus on romantic comedy, Christmas, and cowboys. Plus, I promise a happily ever after. Always.

In my books, you'll only find sweet & swoony romance. That means the intimacy level stops at kissing. There is plenty of sizzle without the spice and no language kids shouldn't hear.

My goals are always to provide a satisfying experience for the reader, honor my Christian faith, and make you laugh and give you the feels. While there are life events featured, my main focus is the relationship between the two main characters.

I have over ten series written or in progress (that amounts to over sixty books), so I try to tie in characters, places, events, and more into each one.

As a reader myself, I get a delighted little thrill when I

read books with interconnected worlds, where characters make cameos, or special events are referenced. It makes me feel connected in a unique way and I hope that for you too!

Speaking of connection, likely, if you read this, you joined my newsletter. (Big thanks!) That's my number one, weekly, spot where I reach out to you in your inbox with all kinds of sweet and swoony goodness, including new release info, sales and freebies, book suggestions, events, giveaways, and more! I welcome emails in response as well and answer every one of them.

You can also find me on Facebook where I have an author page as well as a VIP reader group called Ellie Hall's Sweet and Swoony Fiction Fans. Original, I know. Lol. There, we get personal, interact, and laugh a lot.

Instagram is the other place I hang out and often share stories with my pets, geek out over Bookstagram (that's for those of us who love all things bookish), and where I often ramble on Mondays and Fridays about the writing life.

Thanks again for reading and I hope to connect with you!

If you're looking for your next good read, I encourage you to check out **The Nebraska Knights Holiday Hockey Romance series**: If you enjoyed Gracie and Vohn's romance, you may also like Stupid Cupid, a hate to love, mistaken identity romcom. There is also Redd, Whit & Blue—an enemies to love, single dad, second chance romcom—Love at First Skate, The Kiss Class, and Margo & the Faux Good Luck Beau—all filled with love, laughter, and happily ever afters.

♥Ellie

P.S. If you'd like a paperback copy of The Secret Book

Boyfriend it's available here, at elliehallauthor.com/paper-back and wherever books are sold.

P.P.S. Please consider leaving a review because it helps more readers find my books so I can keep the sweet and swoony romance coming your way!

Also by Ellie Hall

All books are clean and wholesome, Christian faith-friendly and without mature content but filled with swoony kisses and happily ever afters. Books are listed under series in recommended reading order.

-select titles available in audiobook, paperback, hardcover, and large print-

The Only Us Sweet Billionaire Series

Only a Date with a Billionaire

Only a Kiss with a Billionaire

Only a Night with a Billionaire

Only Forever with a Billionaire

Only Love with a Billionaire

Only Christmas with a Billionaire

Only New Year with a Billionaire

The Only Us Sweet Billionaire series box set (books 2-5) + a bonus scene!

Hawkins Family Small Town Romance Series

Second Chance in Hawk Ridge Hollow

Finding Forever in Hawk Ridge Hollow

Coming Home to Hawk Ridge Hollow

Falling in Love in Hawk Ridge Hollow

Christmas in Hawk Ridge Hollow

The Hawk Ridge Hollow Series Complete Collection Box Set (books 1-5)

The Blue Bay Beach Reads Romance Series

Summer with a Marine

Summer with a Rock Star

Summer with a Billionaire

Summer with the Cowboy

Summer with the Carpenter

Summer with the Doctor

Books 1-3 Box Set

Books 4-6 Box Set

Ritchie Ranch Clean Cowboy Romance Series

Rustling the Cowboy's Heart (Book 1)

Lassoing the Cowboy's Heart (Book 2)

Trusting the Cowboy's Heart (Book 3)

Kissing the Christmas Cowboy

Loving the Cowboy's Heart

Wrangling the Cowboy's Heart

Charming the Cowboy's Heart

Saving the Cowboy's Heart

Ritchie Ranch Romance Books 1-4 Box Set

Falling into Happily Ever After Rom Com

An Unwanted Love Story

An Unexpected Love Story

An Unlikely Love Story

An Accidental Love Story

An Impossible Love Story

An Unconventional Christmas Love Story

Forever Marriage Match Romantic Comedy Series

Dare to Love My Grumpy Boss

Dare to Love the Guy Next Door

Dare to Love My Fake Husband

Dare to Love the Guy I Hate

Dare to Love My Best Friend

Home Sweet Home Series

Mr. and Mrs. Fix It Find Love

Designing Happily Ever After

The DIY Kissing Project

The True Romance Renovation: Christmas Edition

Extreme Heart Makeover

Building What's Meant to Be

The Costa Brothers Cozy Christmas Comfort Romance Series

Tommy & Merry and the 12 Days of Christmas

Bruno & Gloria and the 5 Golden Rings

Luca & Ivy and the 4 Calling Birds

Gio & Joy and the 3 French Hens

Paulo & Noella and the 2 Turtle Doves

Nico & Hope and the Partridge in the Pear Tree

The Love List Series

The Swoon List

The Not Love List

The Crush List

The Kiss List

The Naughty or Nice List

Love, Laughs & Mystery in Coco Key

*Clean romantic comedy, family secrets, and treasure *These books should be read in the following order:*

The Romance Situation

The Romance Fiasco

The Romance Game

The Romance Gambit

The Christmas Romance Wish

The Nebraska Knights Holiday Hockey Romance Series

Stupid Cupid

Redd, Whit & Blue

The Kiss Class

Margo & the Faux Good Luck Beau

Love at First Skate (Tie-In)

On the Hunt for Love

Sweet, Small Town & Southern

The Grump & the Girl Next Door

The Bitter Heir & the Beauty

The Secret Son & the Sweetheart

The Ex-Best Friend & the Fake Fiancee

The Best Friend's Brother & the Brain

Don't You Forget About Tea (Tie-In)

SoCal Summer Kisses

We Go Together

The One I Want

Hopelessly Devoted

Stand Alone Titles

Happily Ever Haunted (a romcom - ghost mashup)

Visit www.elliehallauthor.com or your favorite retailer for more.

If you love my books, please leave a review on your favorite retailer's website! Thank you! ♥ Ellie

P.S. I have a clean fantasy and paranormal romance pen name: E. Hall that you might enjoy (best read in listed order):

The Court of Crown and Compass Series

Fae of Light and Shadow (prequel)

Fae of the North (book 1)

Fae of the West (book 2)

Fae of the South (book 3)

Fae of the East (book 4)

RIP Magic Academy Reform School Series

Law & Disorder (book 1)

Crime & Curses (book 2)

Mayhem & Magic (book 3)

Shifter Diaries

Life Fated (book 1)

Lies Tamed (book 2)

Loss Hunted (book 3)

Love United (book 4)

About the Author

Ellie Hall is a USA Today bestselling author. If only that meant she could wear a tiara and get away with it ;) She loves puppies, books, and the ocean. Writing sweet romance with lots of firsts and fizzy feels brings her joy. Oh, and chocolate chip cookies are her fave.
Ellie believes in dreaming big, working hard, and lazy Sunday afternoons spent with her family and dog in gratitude for God's grace.

Do you love sweet, swoony romance?
Stories with happy endings?
Falling in love?
Be sure you're subscribed to my newsletter and say hello and follow me on social media sites, including Facebook, Instagram, YouTube and more @elliehallauthor

facebook.com/elliehallauthor

instagram.com/elliehallauthor

bookbub.com/authors/ellie-hall

Made in United States
North Haven, CT
26 June 2024

54114289R00095